THRAXAS
AND THE
DANCE OF
DEATH

THRAXAS

AND THE

DANCE OF DEATH

MARTIN SCOTT

THRAXAS AND THE DANCE OF DEATH

Copyright © 2002 by Martin Scott. Published by permission of Little, Brown, and Company (UK).

A Baen Book

Baen Publishing Enterprises
P.O. Box 1403
Riverdale, NY 10471
www.baen.com

ISBN-13: 978-1-4165-0907-3
ISBN-10: 1-4165-0907-0

Cover art by Tom Kidd

First U.S. printing, October 2005

Library of Congress Cataloging-in-Publication Data

Scott, Martin, 1956-
  Thraxas and the dance of death / Martin Scott.
    p. cm.
  ISBN-13: 978-1-4165-0907-3
  ISBN-10: 1-4165-0907-0
  1. Private investigators--Fiction. 2. Overweight men--Fiction. 3. Jewelry theft--Fiction.
I. Title.

PR6063.I34T475 2005
823'.92--dc22

                                                                              2005019122

Distributed by Simon & Schuster
1230 Avenue of the Americas
New York, NY 10020

Production by Windhaven Press, Auburn, NH (www.windhaven.com)
Printed in the United States of America

10   9   8   7   6   5   4   3   2   1

THRAXAS
AND THE
DANCE OF
DEATH

Chapter One

It's summer. It's hot. The city stinks. I've just been described as a liar in court and subjected to a stream of hostile invective that would have made a statue flinch. Funds are low, I'm short of work and badly in need of beer. Life, in general, is tough. It's no time for my idiot companion Makri to be complaining about an examination.

"So you have to take an examination. You wanted to go to Guild College. What did you expect?"

"It's not just a written examination. I have to stand up and talk to the whole class. It's making me feel bad."

"You used to fight in the gladiator slave pits. I thought you'd be used to an audience."

Makri shakes her head violently, causing her huge mane

1

of black hair to swing around the small of her back. Underneath all her hair Makri has pointed ears. This often leads to problems.

"That was different. I was killing Orcs. It never felt stressful like talking to a group of students. They're all merchants' sons with money and servants in their houses. They're always laughing at me for being a barmaid. And how am I meant to prepare for anything when this stupid city is as hot as Orcish hell and stinks like a sewer?"

Summer in Turai is never pleasant, and this summer is promising to be as bad as last year when dogs and men keeled over in the street, overcome by the heat, and the main aqueduct into Twelve Seas was dry for a record eighteen days in a row.

Makri continues to complain about her upcoming examination but I'm too annoyed about my recent experience in court to pay attention. A few months ago I arrested a thief down by the docks, name of Baxin. He was stealing Elvish wine. I apprehended him and delivered him, complete with evidence, to the Transport Guild. Unfortunately, being caught in the act of committing a crime has never stopped a Turanian criminal from putting up a strong defence in court. The devious, toga-clad lawyer Baxin hired to defend him made a good job of convincing the jury that Baxin was nothing more than the victim of a bad case of mistaken identity. The real criminal was the notoriously unreliable Investigator Thraxas, a man with a city-wide reputation as a person of bad character.

"Damn it, no one was saying I had a bad character last winter when I saved this city from disgrace. Not to mention helping Lisutaris get elected as head of the Sorcerers Guild. Then it was 'Thank you, Thraxas, you're a hero.'"

"Well, no one actually said that," points out Makri.

"They should have."

"Actually, I seem to remember several Sorcerers saying you should be thrown in prison. And the Deputy Consul was very angry about you turning up drunk on the last day of the Sorcerers Assemblage. And then the Consul threatened—"

"Yes, fine, Makri. You don't need to remind me of every detail of this city's ingratitude. If there was any justice I'd be lounging by a pool in the Palace instead of trudging back to a tavern in the bad part of town."

We walk on through the intolerable heat. Packs of dogs lie listlessly on the baked mud roads and beggars slump in despair at every corner. Welcome to Twelve Seas, home to those city dwellers whose lives have not been going too well. Sailors without a ship, labourers without work, mercenaries without a war, broken-down prostitutes, pimps, thugs, runaways and the rest of the city's underclass all struggling to survive, and no one struggling more than sorcerous Investigator Thraxas—ex-Palace employee, ex-soldier, ex-mercenary, currently broke, ageing, overweight, without prospects and really, really in need of a beer.

"I'm sure that everyone at Guild College doesn't have to give a talk to the class," continues Makri, apparently unaware that I have no interest in her problems. "Professor Toarius is making me do it because he hates me. He just can't stand that I'm a woman. And he can't stand that I've got Orcish blood. Ever since I signed up at the college he's had it in for me. 'Don't do this, don't do that.' Petty restrictions everywhere. 'You can't wear your sword to rhetoric class.' 'Don't threaten your philosophy tutor with an axe.' I tell you, Thraxas, life for me is tough."

"Very tough, Makri. Now please shut up about your damned examination."

It's a long way down Moon and Stars Boulevard from the centre of the city to Twelve Seas. By the time we reach the corner of Quintessence Street I'm sweating like a pig. I'd buy a watermelon from the market if I hadn't lost every guran I had on an unwise investment on a chariot which might possibly have won the race had it not been driven by an Orc-loving charioteer with two left hands and a poor sense of direction.

Down each narrow alleyway youths are dealing dwa, the powerful drug that has the city in its grip. The Civil Guard, bribed or intimidated by the Brotherhood, look the other way. Their customers eye us as we pass, wondering if we might be potential targets for a swift street robbery, but at the sight of the swords at Makri's hips, and my considerable bulk, they look away. No need to tangle with us when there are plenty of easier targets to be found.

The sun beats down cruelly. The crowds around the market stalls kick up clouds of choking dust. By the time we reach the Avenging Axe I'm practically begging for ale. I march through the doors, force my way through the afternoon drinkers and reach for the bar like a drowning man clutching at a rope.

"Beer. Quickly."

The tavern is owned by Gurd, Barbarian from the north, a man I've fought beside all over the world. Recognising the poor state I'm in, he omits the small talk and fills me up a tankard. I down it in one and take another.

"Bad day in court?"

"Very bad. They let Baxin go. So now I'm missing out on the conviction bonus. And you wouldn't believe what the lawyers said about me. I tell you, Gurd, I've about had it with this stinking city. A man can't do an honest day's work without some corrupt court official grinding him into the dust."

My tankard is empty.

"What's the matter? Beer in short supply?"

Gurd hands over a third. He grins. Gurd's around fifty,

and after a life of mercenary wars he's content to settle down peacefully in his tavern. Once a ferocious fighter, he's now a rather mellower person than me. Of course, Gurd had the good sense to save enough money to buy an inn. Everything I ever earned I gambled away, or drank.

By my fourth or fifth beer I'm complaining loudly to all who care to listen that Turai is undoubtedly the worst city in the west.

"I tell you, I've been in Orcish hovels that were more civilised than this place. The next time the city authorities need me to bail them out of a crisis they can forget it. Let them look somewhere else."

The beer doesn't lighten my mood. Even a substantial helping of Tanrose's stew can't cheer me up. As the tavern starts to fill up with dock workers coming off their afternoon shift at the warehouses, I grab another beer and head upstairs. I used to be a Senior Investigator at the Palace with a nice villa in Thamlin. Now I live in two rooms above a tavern. It doesn't make me feel good about my life. Makri lives in another room along the corridor. I bump into her as she emerges. She's changed into her chainmail bikini in readiness for her shift as a waitress.

"Cheered up any?" she asks.

"No."

"Strange. Eight or nine beers usually does it. What's eating you? You've been criticised in court before. Now I think about it, weren't you criticised in the Senate only last year?"

"Yes. I've been lambasted by the best of them. Do you realise that I'm in exactly the same position I was when you arrived in this city a couple of years ago?"

"Drunk?"

"No. I mean broke. Without a coin to my name. Dependent on Gurd for ale on credit till some degenerate walks through my door asking me to investigate some case which will no doubt involve me risking my life for a lousy thirty gurans a day. It's not right. Look what I've done for this city. Fought in the wars, held back the Niojans and repelled the Orcish hordes. Did anyone pin a medal on me for that? Forget it. And who was it saved our necks when Horm the Dead tried to wipe out Turai with his Eight-Mile Terror Spell? Me. Only this winter I got a Turanian elected head of the Sorcerers Guild practically single-handed."

"I helped with that."

"A little. Which doesn't alter the fact that I deserve a lot more than being stuck in this foul tavern. I ought to be employed by the Palace."

"You were employed by the Palace. They bounced you out for being drunk."

"That only goes to prove my point. There's no gratitude. I tell you, if that useless Deputy Consul Cicerius comes down here again begging for help I'm sending him away with a dragon's tooth up his nose. To hell with them all."

"It's not fair," says Makri.

"You're damn right it's not fair."

"I don't see why I have to take this examination. I'm so busy waiting tables I hardly have time to study."

I glare at Makri with loathing. As far as I can see, if a person who's part Elf, part Orc and part Human decides to slaughter her captors, escape to civilisation, then sign up for college, she's only got herself to blame for her problems. She could have remained a gladiator. Makri was good at that. Undefeated champion. She's just about the most savage fighter ever seen in the west, and slaughtering people is her speciality. But Guild College is a foolish enterprise requiring long hours of study in rhetoric, philosophy, mathematics and God knows what else. No wonder she's stressed. The woman—and I use the term loosely—is next door to insane at the best of times; a result, I imagine, of having mixed blood, pointy ears and a general tendency to believe that all of life's difficulties can be solved with violence.

Makri departs downstairs. I take my beer to my room, slam the door, and clear some junk off the couch. I've had enough of this. Poverty is getting me down. I need a plan. There must be a way for a talented man to get ahead in this city. I finish my beer. After a while I drag a bottle of klee out of a drawer and start in on it. The klee burns my throat as it goes down. Finest quality, distilled in the hills. The sun streams in, through the holes in the curtains. My room is hotter than Orcish hell. No one can think in heat like this. I guess I'm just going to finish my days in Twelve Seas broke, angry and unlamented. I finish the klee, toss the bottle in the bin, and fall asleep.

Chapter Two

I'm dreaming about the time I won a beer-drinking contest down in Abelesi. Seven opponents, and every one of them unconscious on the floor while I was still demanding more ale, and quickly. One of my finest moments. I'm rudely awakened by someone shaking my arm. I leap to my feet and make a grab for my sword.

"It's me," says Makri.

I'm angry at the invasion.

"How often do I have to tell you to stay out of my room!" I yell at her. "I swear if you walk in here uninvited again I'll run you through."

"You couldn't run me through if I had both arms tied behind

my back, you fat ox," retorts Makri, never one to smooth over a disagreement.

"One of these days I'm going to break you in half, you skinny troll-lover."

I notice that Makri is not alone.

"You remember Dandelion?"

My heart sinks. It plummets. Even in a city full of strange characters, Dandelion stands out as a particularly odd young woman. She hired me on a case last year, and while I admit this worked out all right in the end, the whole affair didn't endear her to me. Dandelion is weird. Not barbaric like Makri or ethereal like the Elves. Just weird. Not least among the things I dislike about her is her habit of walking around with bare feet, something I'm utterly unable to account for. In a city full of refuse-strewn streets, it defies common sense. You're liable to step on a dead rat, or maybe worse. Besides this she wears a long skirt covered with patterns from the zodiac, and spouts rubbish about communing with nature. She hired me on behalf of the talking dolphins in the bay, which was probably to be expected.

"What do you want?" I grunt. "The talking dolphins having problems again?"

The dolphins don't actually speak Turanian. Just a lot of strange whistles. I saw Dandelion communicating with them but I'm half convinced she was making it up as she went along.

Dandelion tries to smile, but she seems nervous. With my sword in my hand I guess I don't put people at ease. I sheathe it, just in case the woman has anything useful to say. Now I think about it, she did pay me with several valuable antique coins, and I'm not in a position to turn away paying clients no matter how peculiar they might be.

"Dandelion has a warning for you," says Makri.

Makri's keeping a straight face but I sense she's secretly

amused. Springing Dandelion on me when I'm sleeping off ten beers is probably her idea of an excellent joke.

"A warning? From the dolphins?"

Dandelion shakes her head.

"Not from the dolphins. Though they're still very grateful for your assistance. You should visit them some time."

"Next time I need to commune with nature I'll get right down to the beach. What's the warning?"

"You're about to be involved in terrible bloodshed."

Dandelion gazes at me. I gaze back at her. There's a brief silence, interrupted only by the cries of the hawkers outside. At the foot of the steps leading down from my outer door to the street there's an ongoing dispute over territory between a woman who sells fish and a man who's set up a stall for sharpening blades. They've been screaming at each other all week. Life in Twelve Seas is never peaceful.

"Terrible bloodshed? Is that it?"

Dandelion nods. I hunt around for my klee. It's finished.

"I'm an Investigator. I'm always surrounded by bloodshed. Comes with the territory. People round here just don't like being investigated."

"You don't understand," says Dandelion. "I don't mean a little violence. Or even a few deaths. I mean many, many deaths, more deaths than you can count. An orgy of blood-letting such as you've never encountered before."

My head's starting to hurt. The sight of Dandelion with her bare feet and odd clothes is irritating beyond measure. I'd like to bounce her down the stairs.

"Who gave you this warning? The Brotherhood? The Society of Friends?"

"No one gave it me. I read it in the stars."

Makri fails to suppress a giggle. I stare at both of them with loathing.

"You read it in the stars?"

"Yes," says Dandelion, nodding eagerly. "Last night on the beach. I hurried here as fast as I could to warn you. Because I owe you—"

"Will you get out of my office!" I roar. "Makri, how dare you bring this freak in here to bother me like this. If she's still here in five seconds I swear I'll kill you both. Don't you know I'm a busy man? Now get the hell out of here!"

Makri shepherds Dandelion from the room. She pauses at the door.

"Maybe you ought to listen to her, Thraxas. After all, she came up with the goods during the dolphin case."

I tell Makri brusquely I'll be grateful if she never wastes my time again, and add a few curses I usually save for the race track. Makri departs, slamming the door. I open it to curse her again, then sit down heavily. My mood just got a lot worse. I need more sleep. There's a knock on the outside door. I ignore it. It comes again. I continue to ignore it. My outside door is secured by a minor locking spell which is sufficient for keeping out most people, and I'm not in the mood for company. I lie down on my couch just as the door flies open and Lisutaris, Mistress of the Sky, strides into the room. Lisutaris, number one Sorcerer in Turai. Number one Sorcerer in all the Human lands, in fact, since she was elected head of the Sorcerers Guild. She glares down at me.

"Why didn't you answer the door?"

"I was counting on the locking spell to keep out unwanted intruders."

Lisutaris smiles. A locking spell placed by the likes of me is never going to be a problem for such a powerful Sorcerer.

"Are you planning on lying there all day?"

I struggle to rise. Lisutaris is an important woman, and wealthy. She deserves respect, though as I've frequently seen her in a state of collapse due to overindulgence in the narcotic thazis, I don't feel the need to be too formal.

"Do you always greet your clients this way?"

"Only when I'm trying to sleep off the effect of beer. Is this a social call? And incidentally, why are you in disguise?"

"It's a professional call. I'm here to hire you. And I'm in disguise because I don't want anyone to recognise me."

Turai's Sorcerers wear a distinctive rainbow cloak, and as Lisutaris is an aristocratic woman, she'd normally have a fine gown under her cloak, along with jewellery, gold sandals and the like. Instead she's dressed in the plain garb of the lower classes, though any observer could tell that her extravagant hair wasn't coiffured at one of the cheap establishments you'd find in Twelve Seas. Even in a plain robe, Lisutaris, Mistress of the Sky, is a striking woman. She's somewhere around the same age as me, but she's always been an elegant beauty, and careful with her looks.

"I see nothing's changed around here," she says, sweeping some junk off a chair and sitting down lightly. "Is it absolutely necessary for you to live in such squalor?"

"Private investigation never pays that well."

"You were well remunerated for your help at the Sorcerers Assemblage, I believe."

"Not as well remunerated as I should have been. And some recent investments have turned out less well than I antici-pated."

"You mean you lost it all at the chariot races?"

"That's right."

Lisutaris nods.

"I too lost money at the last meeting. Of course, I can afford it. Well, Thraxas, as you're obviously in need of money, I expect you'll be glad to take on the case."

"Tell me about it."

There's a slight delay while Lisutaris lights a thazis stick. She offers me one, which I accept. Thazis is a mild narcotic for most people, but Lisutaris is a very heavy user. She invented a new kind of water pipe and developed a spell for making the plants grow faster. The citizens of Turai are proud that one of our own was recently selected as head of the Sorcerers Guild, but they might be surprised if they knew the full extent of Lisutaris's habit. Generally she's too stoned to walk by the end of the day. She was never that suitable a candidate for head of the Sorcerers Guild really, but there wasn't a better one available, much to the chagrin of Deputy Consul Cicerius. Suitable or not, it was a relief for the Deputy Consul, the Consul and the King to have a Turanian elected. It guarantees us help from all the Sorcerers in the west should we come under attack from the Orcs again, which we will, sooner or later.

"Have you heard of the Sorcerer's green jewel?"

I shake my head.

"I never made it past apprentice. My sorcerous knowledge has a lot of gaps."

"Not many people have heard of it," continues Lisutaris. "It's what you might call a state secret. Even I was unaware of its existence till I became privy to government secrets after my election as head of the Guild. The green jewel is Turai's guarantee against unexpected invasion. In the hands of a powerful Sorcerer, the jewel acts as an all-seeing eye. No matter how private the Orcs might try to keep their affairs, we will always be able to tell when they're massing armies against us. So it's an important piece of rock."

I'm surprised to learn of this artefact, and a little puzzled by Lisutaris's explanation.

"It sounds like a handy thing to have. But what do you mean, it's our only defence against unexpected invasion? The

Sorcerers Guild has plenty of spells for giving us advance warning."

"True. But the Orcish Sorcerers Guild has spent the last fifteen years in a concentrated attempt to negate every one of them. There used to be twenty or more far-seeing spells we could use. Government intelligence now indicates that this is down to two or three. The Orcs have successfully developed counter-spells to the rest. The Orcish Sorcerers Guild is a far more cohesive unit than most things in the east. Even when their states have been riven by internal wars, they've kept working away on the problem. If they come up with counter-spells to our few remaining incantations for tracking their movements, the green jewel will be the only thing standing between the west and oblivion."

This talk of Orcish wars, while uncomfortable, has got my attention. I fought in the last one. So did Lisutaris, Gurd, and practically every other able-bodied Turanian who was old enough to wield a blade or chant a spell. In the climax of a savage and destructive conflict we threw them back from the walls, but it was a close thing till the Elves arrived from the south. Without their aid, Turai would now be an outpost of the Orcish empire, or a pile of ruins.

"So the Orcish Sorcerers have been busy and we're now dependent on the green jewel."

"That's right," says Lisutaris. "I trust I've impressed you with the great importance of this item?"

"You have. So what about it?"

"It was entrusted to me."

"And?"

"I lost it."

"You lost it? How?"

"I put it in my bag when I went to the chariot races. Which was not as careless as it might sound. To use the jewel properly, it's necessary for a Sorcerer to become very familiar with it, and learn its properties in all circumstances. Unfortunately when I returned home it was no longer in my bag. I think it may have dropped out when I was giving my secretary some money to place a bet."

"What chariot?"

"City Destroyer."

"Bad choice. I lost a bundle on that."

"The jewel was—"

"Didn't you think there was something fishy about the way it dropped out of the running on the last lap? I think the charioteer may have been bribed."

"Of course I looked for it at the time but—"

"I'm not convinced that Melus the Fair was the right choice for Stadium Sorcerer. I'm sure there's some corruption going on that she's not picking up on—"

Lisutaris informs me coldly that she didn't come here to discuss our mutual misfortunes at the races.

"I've just lost the most important weapon in the nation's armoury and I need it back quickly. If word of this gets out, the King will have me expelled from the city, or possibly something worse. So I'd appreciate it if you'd start investigating without further delay."

"No need to get upset. I was just sharing in your misfortunes. City Destroyer should have won that race at a canter. It's getting so a man can't make an honest bet these days."

I notice that the Mistress of the Sky has a threatening glint in her eye. I get down to business.

"You'll need to tell me some more details."

"The green jewel is set in a pendant, Elvish silverwork, quite distinctive. However, I do not require you to do much investigating. Though I was unable to find the pendant immediately—you will understand that I did not wish to draw attention to my loss by performing a spell at the Stadium Superbius under the nose of Consul Kalius—as soon as I returned home I put my powers to use. I have now located the pendant by means of sorcery. It's being held in a tavern next to the harbour. The Spiked Mace. Are you familiar with it?"

"Yes. It's the sort of place you'd expect stolen jewels to end up."

"So I imagined. You will understand, Thraxas, that absolute secrecy is necessary. I cannot allow the King, the Consul or any of my fellow Sorcerers to learn that I have lost the jewel. That being the case, I am unable to stride into the tavern myself and start blasting people with spells. Explanations would be called for which I would be unwilling to provide."

I understand well enough. In a city which hates and fears the Orcs, anyone found to have carelessly lost our most powerful protection against them would soon find their life not worth living. It is a shocking piece of carelessness on Lisutaris's part, though in truth it's not surprising. Her thazis habit is so severe that bad things were bound to happen once she ended up head of the Guild.

"Why didn't you just send someone from your household?"

"I deem it too much of a risk. Even if they were not recognised there is no telling who might later learn of the affair. Turanian servants are not known for their discretion. My secretary is of course absolutely loyal, but she is a young woman of rather delicate constitution and not suitable for a task such as this. Though I know the address where you may find the jewel, I do not know what else you might find there."

"Someone who really doesn't want to return it, most likely. The Spiked Mace is the original den of thieves. Don't worry, I'll get it back."

From Lisutaris's description of events, it seems quite possible that the thief won't realise what he's got. He may believe he's holding nothing more than a normal piece of dress jewellery and try to sell it as soon as possible for a modest profit.

Lisutaris shifts uncomfortably in the sticky heat of my office. During the winter the Mistress of the Sky, like every other Sorcerer, had warming spells on her apparel to fight off the bitter cold, but cooling oneself by sorcery is far more difficult. A worried expression flits across her face.

"Given that discretion is essential, you won't start throwing your legal powers around, will you?"

I frown. I've been busy trying to forget that I had any legal powers. After many years as a private citizen, I was unexpectedly elevated to the position of Tribune of the People some months ago by Cicerius, the Deputy Consul. The Tribunate, a sort of official citizens' representative, was an extinct post till Cicerius nominated me last winter. He did this purely so I would be granted access to the Sorcerers Assemblage. It was never his intention, or mine, that I'd actually do anything official, but I was blackmailed into using my Tribune's powers to halt an eviction, something which carried with it various political ramifications. Since I'm always keen to avoid getting involved in Turai's murky political world, I've been playing down the Tribune bit as much as possible ever since, and have flatly refused to use the authority of the position again, knowing that it will only land me in trouble with some powerful party or other.

"Don't worry. The post was purely honorary. Senator Lodius forced me into action once, but that's it."

The position lasts for a year and I'm hoping that the last few months of my term will run out unnoticed by all, leaving me once more a private citizen. A man who goes around using political power in Turai needs a lot more protection than I've got.

Lisutaris lights another thazis stick.

"You didn't gamble the jewel away, did you?"

She has the good grace to smile.

"No. I'm still wealthy. However, if the loss is made public, you will not be the only person to make that remark. The Stadium Superbius was an unfortunate place to lose the pendant and there has been some jealousy in certain circles since I was elected head of the Guild."

Lisutaris takes out her purse and lays some money on the table.

"Thirty gurans. Your standard retainer, I believe. There's one more thing. I positively must have the jewel back quickly. In four days' time I'm holding a masked ball at my mansion and the Crown Prince will be there, along with Kalius and Cicerius. It is entirely likely that they will wish to view the jewel. Consul Kalius was, I know, somewhat dubious about letting me take it from the Palace."

I'm not surprised. Anyone who saw Lisutaris stumbling around the Sorcerers Assemblage in a thazis-induced stupor would have been dubious about letting her take anything valuable home with her.

"Couldn't you cancel the ball?"

Apparently not. Lisutaris's masked ball is set to be a highlight of the social season. I wonder what it's like to have a social season.

"I'll get it back."

"When you have it, be certain not to stare into it."

"Why not?"

"It's a powerful sorcerous object. Handling the pendant for a short space of time is quite safe, but it could be hazardous for an untrained person to gaze deeply into the green jewel. It may induce fainting, or worse."

"I'll put it straight into my pocket."

Lisutaris is now on to her third thazis stick. She finishes it, drops the end in my bin, and lights another.

"How is Makri?"

Lisutaris is acquainted with Makri; she hired her to be her bodyguard at the Sorcerers Assemblage.

"Same as usual. Busy and bad-tempered."

"I have something for her."

The Sorcerer hands me an envelope. Makri's name is written on it in the fancy script of a professional scribe. I promise to pass it on. I'm curious, but I figure it's none of my business, so after Lisutaris leaves I dump it in Makri's room. Then I douse myself with water to get rid of the last effects of the alcohol and thazis, and strap on my sword. Finally I load one spell—the most I can comfortably manage—into my memory and head out into the streets. Outside, the knife sharpener and the fish vendor are still arguing. It's bound to end in violence.

Chapter Three

At the foot of the stairs, I run into Moxalan, younger son of Honest Mox the bookmaker. Only son I should say, as his older sibling succumbed to an overdose of dwa last winter, around the same time that Minarixa the baker also died of an overdose. I miss the baker terribly. Life isn't the same without her pastries. I don't miss Mox's son, but as I do a lot of trade with the bookmaker, it's as well to be civil to his family.

Moxalan is around nineteen, open-faced and friendly, not yet having taken on the mean and cunning look of the hardened bookmaker. His tunic is plain but well cut and his sandals are expensive enough to let anyone know that his father's business isn't doing badly. We exchange greetings and he tells me that he's here to ask Makri for help with some theories of architecture, which makes no sense to me.

"Theories of architecture?"

"For the Guild College. We're in the same class. I missed a lecture so I want Makri's notes."

I didn't know Honest Mox was sending his younger son to Guild College, though it's not really a surprise. A man who's raking in as much cash as Mox can afford the fees, and Mox, as a bookmaker, has very low social status in the city. It's not uncommon for men of low status who find themselves wealthy to try and improve the family lot by educating their sons and getting them into the civil service, or something similar.

"Not entering the family business, then?"

He shakes his head.

"I help out a little, but my father wants me to better myself. Is Makri in the tavern?"

"Yes. She's working."

Moxalan is confident that Makri will have a full set of notes from the course.

"She's the best student. Much better than me. Did you know she's top of every class?"

I didn't. Makri probably mentioned it but I don't pay that much attention. I notice that Moxalan's face goes a little dopey as he mentions Makri's name. I recognise the symptom. Young men, on seeing Makri's impressive figure crammed into two barely adequate strips of chainmail, tend to forget that their mothers want them to marry a sensible girl from a good family and their fathers warned them to stay away from women with Orcish blood. Even the Elves were impressed, and it's next door to taboo for Elves to be impressed by anything remotely connected to the Orcs. What these young men don't realise is that their mothers were right. Life with Makri would be hell, no matter how fabulous they think her figure is. She'll never shake off the effects of growing up as a gladiator. At the first sign of a domestic argument, Makri would very likely behead her husband and paint her face with his blood.

"I thought she'd be with you," says Moxalan.

"Why?"

"Because of the warning."

Again I don't know what he's talking about. Moxalan explains that he's heard about Dandelion warning me of a bloodbath. In a place like Twelve Seas, rumours travel fast. I'm aggravated, and not just because I don't like my private business becoming the stuff of gossip. The implication seems to be that if I'm heading into danger I need Makri to protect me. As if I didn't get along fine for years before she arrived.

"Don't worry about me," I grunt, and take my leave.

The Spiked Mace is an unpleasant little establishment close to the harbour, full of drunken sailors and unruly stevedores. Unlike many of the local taverns, it's not owned by the Brotherhood, the criminal gang that controls most of the crime south of the river. Which is good news for me. If I tried to remove stolen loot from the Brotherhood, they'd be down on me like a bad spell. Most likely I'll find the pendant in the hands of some petty thief who'll be keen to sell it as soon as possible to raise money for his next dose of dwa. If the guy is desperate enough and lets me have it cheap, I might even make a profit on the deal. Hell, Lisutaris isn't going to gripe over a few gurans, not with the wealth she has, and her huge villa in Thamlin. It's a simple job and shouldn't involve much thought, which is just as well, as the heat makes thinking an arduous business.

As usual, contact with a member of the Turanian aristocracy has left me envious of their wealth. I've always been poor. A few years ago I worked my way up to a nice job as Senior Investigator at the Palace, with a big office, a nice home and lackeys to do the work. Then I drank myself out of the job. My father always said I'd come to nothing. So far I've been unable to prove him wrong.

The sun beats down. The streets are as hot as Orcish hell, and inside the Spiked Mace it's worse. The heat mingles with the smell of rancid ale and burning dwa. Thazis smoke drifts over the tables. The wooden beams overhead are blackened with age. The prostitute who patrols the area with red ribbons in her hair strives vainly to interest the largely inebriated clientele. There's a woman on the floor who looks like she might be dead. I shake my head. This is about as low as life gets. No civilised person would visit this tavern.

"Thraxas! We were wondering where you'd got to."

I come here occasionally. Mainly in the line of business. The barman, and owner of the establishment, is Gavarax, one-time captain of his own fighting trireme till he was kicked out of the navy for failing to hand over booty to the King. He's dark-skinned and has a scar stretching from chin to eyebrow, a result of some naval encounter which he's not shy of bragging about when the old salts get to remembering the old days. Taking a beer merely to be polite, I ask him if there's been anyone in trying to sell a stolen jewel. Gavarax isn't the sort of man who'd give information to the Civil Guard, but he knows me well enough to pass on anything that won't get him into trouble, providing there's something in it for him.

Gavarax waits till the customer at the bar—a docker, from his red bandanna, but not one who's planning on working in the next week or two—departs unsteadily with his drink before leaning over to inform me quietly that actually, yes, there was a man of that sort. I slide a few gurans over the bar.

"He's upstairs now in the private room. With a couple of others. Never seen them before."

I make to leave. Gavarax grabs my arm.

"If you're going to kill anyone, go easy on the furniture."

Making my way through the smoky, noisy room to the stairs at the back, I'm thinking that this case is going to be even easier than I anticipated. I climb the stairs and wait outside the room, listening. Not a sound. I boot the door open and march in, sleep spell ready, in case anyone is planning on resisting.

There are four men in the room, but they're not going to do much resisting. Three of them are dead and the other one looks like he'll be joining them soon. Each one stabbed. It makes for a very large puddle of blood. I bend over the only one who's still breathing, albeit shallowly.

"What happened?"

He tries to look at me, but his eyes won't focus.

"I was on a beautiful golden ship," he whispers. Then he coughs up some blood and dies.

As last words go, they're fairly strange. I file them away for later consideration and look round the room. The window at the back is open and there's blood on the sill. There's an alleyway outside and it's not too far to the ground. No problem making a getaway, though I'm wondering quite what sort of person it was who got away. Obviously a person or persons capable of taking care of themselves. The dead men are all wearing swords. Petty thieves aren't necessarily trained fighters, but it's never that easy to kill four armed opponents.

Moving quickly, I start searching the bodies. They're still warm. I've handled plenty of corpses in my time but I don't enjoy it. I recognise one of them. Axaten, a petty thief, often worked at the Stadium Superbius, picking up whatever he could from careless race-goers. I don't recognise the other three. None of them has the pendant. All I find are a few coins in their purses. No tattoos, nothing identifying them as belonging to any organisation. I search the room, again without results.

I look down into the alley. An easy enough drop for a lighter person maybe, but with my bulk I'm not keen to try it out. Besides, there's the matter of four corpses to consider. I'd like nothing better than to leave them here and sneak out, but there's no point. Gavarax isn't going to cover for me. As soon as the bodies are found, he'll squeal to the Civil Guard and I'll be a handy suspect for murder.

I curse mightily and retrace my steps downstairs to the bar. Gavarax isn't pleased.

"Four of them? All dead? The guards are going to love this."

His eyes narrow.

"Did you kill them?"

"I'm not that quick with a sword these days."

Gavarax glances at my belly. He can believe it. He sends a boy off with a message and I wait in the dingy tavern for the guards to arrive. I'm now in for what will undoubtedly be an uncomfortable interrogation. I'm going to have more than a few words to say to Lisutaris, Mistress of the Sky.

Chapter Four

Approximately nine hours after finding the bodies, I climb out of a horse-drawn landus, pay the driver, and head up the long, long pathway to Lisutaris's villa. I've had six hours of questioning from the Civil Guard and two hours' sleep, and I'm not in what you'd call a good mood. The sight of Lisutaris's beautifully tended flower beds, trees and bushes doesn't make things any better. People with this sort of money generally don't find themselves on the wrong end of six hours' hostile questioning by a series of Guards, each one dumb as an Orc and none of them looking like they'd mind knocking me around the room if I didn't come up with some better answers. If Captain Rallee hadn't appeared they probably would have. The Captain doesn't like me, but he only uses violence against suspects in emergencies. The Guards don't actually think I killed the four men in the Spiked Mace. Not Captain Rallee anyway, he knows me better, though some of his superiors think I'm capable of anything. Prefect Galwinius, head of the Guard in Twelve Seas, would like nothing better than to send me off to a slave galley. Rallee's more sensible, but the problem is that I can never bring myself to tell the Guards too much about any case I'm working on. No matter how many times the Captain demanded that I tell him what I was doing in the Mace, I just wasn't going to say that I was there looking for a pendant for Lisutaris. If I started identifying my clients every time I ran into trouble, I'd soon run out of clients.

Eventually Captain Rallee let me go, with the warning that he'd be down on me like a bad spell if I found myself in the vicinity of any more corpses on his beat. After assuring him that I'd endeavour to stay well clear of anyone dead, I took a hurried breakfast at the Avenging Axe and headed off to see Lisutaris. By the time I reach the front door—a very fancy affair, with a portal, engravings and gold fittings—I'm madder than a mad dragon and relishing the opportunity of batting some minion out of the way. Unfortunately the door is answered by a servant I've met several times previously, and she ushers me straight in.

"I'll tell the Mistress you're here," she says, politely, and vanishes before I can think of a reason to fire off an angry retort.

I'm in a room overlooking the grounds at the back of the villa. Vast, extensive gardens. More trees, flowers, bushes and landscaped pathways than a man would know what to do with, plus private fish pools and an orchard which Lisutaris treats with sorcery to produce fresh fruit out of season. Last month she hosted a garden party for the city's Elvish ambassadors.

It was delightful. So I read anyway. There wasn't any danger of me being invited.

The Mistress of the Sky drifts into the room. She's smiling, slightly vacantly. Lisutaris always starts early with her water pipe.

"Thraxas. This is very quick work. Congratulations."

"I don't have the pendant."

"You don't?"

"No. But I have four dead bodies and an even closer acquaintance with the Civil Guard."

I fill her in on yesterday's events. She's displeased to learn of my failure.

"So you don't know who these men were?"

"I recognised one of them. Axaten. Petty thief, works the stadium, or used to before he got his throat cut. Might well be the person who stole the pendant. I didn't know the other three and I don't know who killed them. I was hoping you might tell me."

Lisutaris looks blank.

"What do you mean?"

"I mean you sent me to get back a jewel from a thief and I ended up in a slaughterhouse. Any idea why that might be?"

"No."

"Do the words 'I was on a beautiful golden ship' mean anything to you?"

"No. Is it a quotation?"

"I don't know. I never studied the great poets. But they were said to me by a dying man. I've seen plenty of dying men but no one ever used that particular phrase before."

I look meaningfully at Lisutaris. She doesn't like the meaning.

"Are you suggesting I may have withheld information from you?"

"Well, have you?"

Lisutaris rises from her chair.

"Thraxas. I appreciated your help during the election. But possibly our close contact at that time has left you with the erroneous impression that you're free to come into my house and call me a liar. You are not."

The Mistress of the Sky looks threatening. I tell her to calm down. She claps her hands and a servant enters carrying her thazis pipe on a tray.

"That's calmer than I intended. Can't you lay off that stuff for a single day?"

Lisutaris doesn't deign to answer this. She makes me wait while she goes through the ritual of filling her pipe and lighting it. As she inhales for the first time, she rubs one gold-sandalled foot over the other, signifying pleasure, maybe.

"Surely there are any number of reasons why those men might have been killed? In a place like that?"

"True. Arguments among thieves can quickly turn murderous in Twelve Seas. But I don't like it that they were killed while they just happened to be in possession of such a valuable item. You're saying that no one knows what this jewel does, but the way it looks to me, someone does. Either the person who stole it, or whoever's got it now. And that makes the whole thing a lot more difficult."

"No one else could know the true value of that pendant." Lisutaris is adamant. "Its use is known only to the King, his senior ministers and the head of the Sorcerers Guild."

"Turai is corrupt from top to bottom. And there are a lot of people very well versed in digging out secrets, particularly when there's a profit involved. How about your own household?"

"No one here knew of the pendant's true purpose, apart from my secretary, who knows all my affairs and is entirely trustworthy."

"I'd like to talk to her."

Lisutaris shakes her head.

"You will not speak to my secretary. You may take it from me that she is not a suspect in this matter."

Lisutaris draws deeply on the thazis pipe. It was bad enough losing the pendant to a petty thief. If it's ended up in the hands of some gang who'll sell it to the highest bidder she's in big trouble, especially if the highest bidder turns out to be one of the Orcish nations. She pulls a slender cord that hangs by the door, summoning a servant.

"I will locate the jewel again and you must retrieve it immediately."

"Are you sure you don't want to bring someone else in? Palace security, for instance? Maybe it's time to let the Consul know what's happened."

"If Kalius finds out about this he'll be down on me like a bad spell. I'm not ready to be expelled from the city just yet."

A servant arrives carrying a golden bowl of an inky-black liquid, kuriya. In this pool a good Sorcerer can often see versions of events both past and present. I've used it myself, with difficulty. These days I find it very hard to reach the required levels of concentration. Such is Lisutaris's power that she requires no preparation. She simply flutters her hand over the liquid and a picture starts to form.

"Another tavern," mutters the Sorceress. "The Mermaid. Do you know it?"

"I do. And it's probably bad news. The Mermaid is run by the Brotherhood."

"So?"

"Getting a jewel back from that organisation is a lot harder than getting it back from a petty thief. Still, there's always the chance that they really don't know what they're handling. If it's just ended up there as a result of some argument among thieves rather than been taken there as an item of great value, I still might be able to retrieve it. Might mean making a larger payment, but if I pretend it's a family heirloom which the owner is desperate to get back, there's no reason for them not to believe me. I know Casax, the local boss. He might be willing to sell me the jewel. He knows I'm not going to report the matter to the authorities."

Lisutaris summons another servant and instructs her to bring me a bag of fifty guran pieces.

"Get it back. No matter what it costs."

I notice that some workers have arrived in the garden outside and are putting up a large marquee.

"Preparations for the masked ball?"

Lisutaris nods.

"I must have the pendant back before the ball. I am certain that the Consul will ask about it. Did Makri get her invitation?"

"What?"

"Her invitation," repeats Lisutaris.

"You invited Makri?"

"Yes. After all, she did excellent service for me as my bodyguard at the Sorcerers Assemblage. I felt she deserved some further reward. In addition I have promised to introduce her to the Professor of Mathematics at the Imperial University."

"What for? Nothing is going to make the University take Makri as a student."

"Probably not," agrees Lisutaris. "However, she will enjoy the ball."

I stare out at the huge marquee. The workers, efficient in a way you rarely see in Twelve Seas, have already got it into shape and are carrying in tables, chairs and candlesticks. The servant returns with my bag of gold coins. Another servant leads me out to the carriage Lisutaris is providing for my journey.

The situation with the pendant is now extremely serious. It's going to take some clever work to retrieve it. However, I'm not thinking about this. I'm thinking about the gross injustice of Makri, Barbarian gladiator who hardly knows how to use a fork or a spoon, being invited to Lisutaris's smart party. No sign of an invitation for me, of course. Don't worry about Thraxas. He'll slog his way round town, fighting criminals and facing danger to get you out of a hole. He'll sit around in a Guards' cell for six hours, protecting your good name. Doesn't mean you have to invite him to your party. I'm quite happy drinking in the Avenging Axe in Twelve Seas with the rest of the struggling masses. Damn Lisutaris. I never liked the woman.

South of the river, my driver starts getting nervous. His duties for Lisutaris don't normally take him to this sort of place. In the sweltering heat it seems to take for ever to work our way through the heavy traffic of wagons on their way to the harbour. When he finally offloads me in Twelve Seas, he spurs his horses and departs as swiftly as he can, pleased to be on his way.

"Thanks for the lift," I mutter, and head into the Avenging Axe. Urgent business or not, I can't visit the Mermaid before eating something. I could do with a beer as well. Lisutaris broke out the wine for me, but these fine Elvish vintages don't satisfy a man.

Outside the tavern I again run into Moxalan. He's in conversation with old Parax, the shoemaker.

"Was there much of a bloodbath?" asks Parax, which is quite an odd question.

I shrug.

"Many deaths?"

"That's private business. And what do you care?"

"We're concerned about you," says Parax.

If old Parax is concerned about me, it's the first I've heard about it. I wonder what the bookmaker's son is still hanging around for. He must have got his architecture notes by now. Possibly he's come back to see Makri again, poor fool that he is.

Suddenly violent shouting erupts from inside the tavern. I hurry in to find the place in chaos. Makri, axe in hand, is attempting to leave while Gurd and Tanrose are trying to hold her back. Several tables are overturned and the lunchtime drinkers are cowering in the corners. From the look of things I'd say it's been quite a struggle. Makri is a demon in a sword fight, but Gurd's a strong man and he's managed to drag Makri to a halt. Not wishing to actually kill her employer, she twists round to face him.

"Gurd, I'm warning you. Let go of me now."

Despite her skinny frame and Gurd's immense strength, Makri is quite capable of beating him in combat if she gets angry enough to use her weapons. Gurd knows this. He doesn't let go. I hurry forward and force my way in between them.

"What the hell is going on?"

"She's going to kill everyone at the Guild College," explains Tanrose.

I blink.

"What?"

"You heard her," snarls Makri, and wrenches herself free to head for the door. I hurl myself after her.

"Makri. Come back. It's only an examination. Don't take it so personally."

"It's not the examination," growls Makri, and disappears through the door.

I look to Gurd for an explanation.

"She's been expelled for theft," he says.

I rush out into the street. In these circumstances Makri really will slaughter everyone. Damn the woman and her temper, I don't have time for this. I catch up with her on the corner, trampling over a beggar who picked this unfortunate moment to accost her.

"Makri, instead of marching up Quintessence Street waving your axe, how about telling me what's going on?"

Makri halts. There's a look of murderous rage in her eyes I haven't seen since the last time I insulted her ears.

"Some money went missing from the students' common room. Professor Toarius says I took it. He's expelled me. Now get out of my way while I go and kill him."

"What do you mean, he says you took it? Was there an investigation?"

"So he claims. Get out of my way."

"Stop telling me to get out of the way. Don't you think it might be better for someone to sort this out rather than you just killing the Professor? They'll arrest you and hang you."

"No they won't. I'll kill everyone who tries and then I'll leave the city."

"Well, that would be an alternative plan."

A dog starts sniffing round Makri's ankles. She kicks it. It goes away whimpering. The way Makri is brandishing her axe it's lucky to still have its head.

Despite the fact that Makri is barbaric, annoying and unreasonable, not to mention part Orc, she's one of the very few friends I have in this city. And while I'm not going to come out and admit it in public, she's been a lot of help in some of my recent cases. I'd possibly regret it if she was hanged.

"Tell me what happened."

Makri screws up her face. Not hastening to kill someone who's accused her of theft is taking a lot of effort.

"I went in to college this morning. For my class in rhetoric. I had to go to the common room to leave my bag because

I had two knives with me and they don't let me take them into class."

"Why did you have two knives with you?"

"Why not?"

"Foolish question. Go on."

"There are some lockers. I have a key. I locked my knives away then I went to my class. We were learning how to make a speech in court. About halfway through the lesson a student came in and said the Professor wanted to see me. Which was unusual. Normally he tries to avoid me. So I went along to his office and he said that another student had lost some money from the common room and I'd been seen taking it! And then he expelled me!"

Makri's voice has been rising throughout this and as she finishes she's almost overcome with emotion. People stare at us, though not as much as they would have a year or so ago. The sight of Makri walking along Quintessence Street heavily armed is something the locals have become used to. As a woman with Orcish blood she's not exactly popular, but people know better than to get in her way.

"Makri. Go home. I'll fix things. I know the Professor has it in for you. No doubt after the money went missing he was keen to jump to conclusions."

"How dare he accuse me of theft!"

It is unjust. Makri is relentlessly honest. Gets me down at times.

"Yes, how dare he. But do you really want to be chased out of the city? After all the work you've done here? What about your plan to go to the Imperial University?"

"You laugh at that plan. Everybody laughs at it."

I'm starting to feel frustrated. At this moment I should be recovering a valuable jewel for Lisutaris, not helping a waitress with her career options.

"Of course I laugh at it. It's impossible. But you've managed to do other impossible things since you arrived, so what the hell, maybe you'll manage this one. So stop threatening to kill your professor, and come back into the Avenging Axe. I'll go to the College, find out what's going on, and sort it out."

Makri stares at me for a long time. It's alien to her nature to let another person fix a problem for her.

"Lisutaris is planning to introduce you to a professor at the university," I point out.

"Can you fix it today?" demands Makri.

"I can try."

"If you fix it today then it's okay. If not, I swear I'll kill Toarius tomorrow, and every other person at the college if I feel like it."

Makri spins on her heel to march back into the tavern. Then, as if remembering something, she spins round again.

"What's happening on the case you're working on?"

"It's gone bad."

"Anyone dead?"

"Yes."

"How many?"

I stare at her.

"What do you mean, how many?"

"I just wondered."

"Four, if you must know. Why is everyone suddenly interested in my business?"

Makri marches back into the tavern. Not having had the chance to fill up on beer, I follow her. I head for the bar with a determined expression on my face, warning everyone to stay out of my path. Unfortunately this has no effect on Dandelion, who appears from nowhere and practically throws herself in front of me.

"I have terrible news," she wails.

"If it's something to do with the stars, I'm not interested."

"You must listen!"

"Can it wait till I get a beer?"

Apparently not. There's no putting the woman off. Dandelion is practically jumping up and down in her frenzied eagerness to tell me something.

"They're betting on the result. Even though I told them it was wrong."

She's lost me completely here.

"What are you talking about?"

"Everyone is laying bets on how many deaths there are going to be in the case you're working on! It's because I warned you there was going to be a bloodbath! A bookmaker has been here and they're taking bets!"

"Dandelion!" says Makri, loudly. "Don't distract Thraxas with your fanciful stories. He's a busy man."

"She gets these strange ideas," says Gurd, and looks guilty.

I stare at the pair of them.

"Is this true?"

"First I've heard about it," says Makri. "Shouldn't you be on your way to the College to clear me of theft?"

"That can wait. I wondered why you were so keen to know the exact body count."

Makri contrives to look innocent.

"I wouldn't place a bet on such a tragedy as four deaths," she says, in a dignified manner.

"Four?"

It's Parax, who's been listening in the background. "Did you say four? Already?"

He turns to Moxalan.

"I want to raise my bet."

There are some mutters of interest from various onlookers who seem to be heavily involved already.

"We could be looking at double figures," says one of them.

I'm furious.

"Is the whole tavern in on this? I can't believe you'd all stoop so low!" I cry, taking in Gurd, Makri and the assembled lowlifes in one sweeping stare.

"Couldn't you just have stayed quiet, you idiot?" says Makri to Dandelion.

"Don't pick on Dandelion," I roar. "She's the only honest person in the place. Makri, I'm appalled at you."

A vocal faction want to know if it's true that the Sorcerers Guild has declared war on the Brotherhood.

"If they start throwing spells around we could be talking about fifty deaths. Maybe more."

"If Thraxas gets killed, do we keep on counting?" demands Parax of Moxalan.

"No. It's clearly stated in the rules that Thraxas's death ends the body count."

"What rules?" I demand

"The rules of the contest. Hey, don't look at me like that, Thraxas. I'm a bookmaker's son. Just because I'm going to college doesn't mean I've left the business."

I shake my head. Sweat is pouring down my tunic. I never expected to find any trace of ethics among the clientele of the Avenging Axe, but even I'm surprised at this. It's immoral. Taking bets on how many deaths there are going to be in my current case? What's that going to do for my reputation?

I curse everyone roundly. So irate am I that I actually march out of the tavern without picking up a beer and I can't remember the last time I did that. I need to get to the Mermaid to recover the pendant as quickly as possible, so I set off at a brisk pace, promising myself that I'll have more than a few harsh words for Makri and Gurd when I get back.

Youthful dwa dealers hover round the alleyway that leads to the Mermaid. Close by are customers in various states of consciousness. Even in the open air the heavy aroma of burning dwa is easily discernible. The situation with this narcotic has now got completely out of hand. Ten years ago the local youths would have been stealing fruit from the market. Now they're knifing strangers in the back for a few gurans. The violence of the gangs that control the trade has increased in proportion to the profits involved. The huge increase in illegal profits has led to city-wide corruption on unheard-of levels. Turai is a mess. It's not just the Orcs we need protecting from.

Lisutaris hired me to retrieve her pendant. I've failed once and I don't intend to fail again. I march towards the Mermaid ready to look Casax, the Brotherhood boss, squarely in the eye and demand the return of the jewel. This doesn't work out so well. Before I reach the door it bursts open and Casax, Karlox and about twenty of their associates rush out of the building, pursued by smoke and flames. The Mermaid is about to burn to the ground. I shake my head. It's turning into another really bad day.

Chapter Five

With its hot, dry summers, Turai is prone to serious outbreaks of fire. Fortunately, the city's fire-fighting services are well advanced. The best in the civilised world, some say. Given that much of the land is covered with tall wooden buildings crammed close to their neighbours, nothing else will do. Since half the city burned down around seventy years ago, there's been a sustained effort to improve our fire-fighting capabilities, and thanks to a series of decrees from the Senate, the Prefect who runs each district is obliged to provide and maintain a sufficient number of water-carrying wagons, complete with equipment and emergency personnel to man them. This served us well during the last war, when the Orcish armies besieging Turai hurled fireballs over the walls with their siege devices but failed to destroy the city as intended. Around that time an engineer in the army developed an efficient new type of water pump which, in the hands of operators strong enough to keep the pistons moving, is capable of throwing water almost fifty yards. Equipped with this device, our fire-fighters have in recent years performed heroic service and are one of the few groups of people universally admired in Turai.

As the tavern empties and smoke starts to billow out of the windows, a great cry goes up for the fire services. A bell is sounded in alarm and people look to the end of the alleyway, anxiously expecting horse-drawn wagons to appear. Nothing happens. No wagons come. As Casax the Brotherhood boss sees his headquarters starting to disappear in flames, he becomes agitated. He screams for his men to bring water from neighbouring houses, waving his fists to encourage them. The way the flames are taking hold, I doubt that this is going to do much good.

Normally I'd enjoy seeing the Mermaid burning to the ground. However, it strikes me that it's hardly helpful to my immediate purposes. I approach Casax. He doesn't acknowledge me, being too busy trying to save the tavern to pay any attention to an unwelcome Investigator. I grab him by the arm.

"Aren't you forgetting something, Casax?"

I point to a young guy in a fancy cloak who's slumped in the alleyway, suffering either from inhaling smoke or, more probably from shock at finding himself dragged out of a burning building in the nick of time.

"Your pet Sorcerer."

"What?"

"Orius. Or, to give him his full name, Orius Fire Tamer. Which name leads me to suspect he ought to be able to do something."

Casax wastes no time. In seconds he's dragging the unfortunate young man up on to his feet and over to the fire.

"Put it out!" screams Casax.

Orius looks like he'd rather be elsewhere, concentrating on his recovery, and struggles to stand erect. I can't say I'm sympathetic. I never thought it was a good idea for the young Sorcerer to get involved with the Brotherhood. Life for a gang member has its rewards, but it can be tough at times.

Just when it seems that the flames must engulf the tavern, Orius manages to catch his breath and gather his concentration. He chants a spell. The flames seem to weaken. He chants again, and they go out. The crowd cheer. Orius Fire Tamer collapses in a heap. To give him his due, it was a nice piece of sorcery, in difficult circumstances.

Casax doesn't waste any time congratulating his Sorcerer. He needs to see that his headquarters have survived intact, so he strides swiftly into the tavern, motioning his henchmen to follow. I walk in after them, uninvited. The building hasn't fared too badly. Part of the roof has collapsed, but Orius halted the flames before they really took hold. Coughing from the effects of the smoke that still hangs in the air, I look around. I don't quite know what I'm looking for and I don't get much of a chance to search before Casax spots me and angrily demands to know what I'm doing here.

"Just visiting. And incidentally, you owe me for reminding you about Orius Fire Tamer."

"I'll send you a present," rasps Casax. "Now get out of here."

"You want to tell me how the fire started?"

"I don't want to tell you anything. Maybe you should be telling me something."

I shake my head.

"All I know is that Prefect Galwinius has been

pocketing the money he should've been spending on fire wagons."

"So what are you doing here? I get suspicious when Investigators turn up just when my building is burning down."

Casax stares at me. I stare back at him. We've had a few run-ins in the past. Nothing too serious. Nothing to make us lifelong friends. All around, Brotherhood men are dampening down the last few tongues of flame and carrying boxes here and there, presumably illicit goods, or maybe Casax's records. Casax is an organised sort of guy. All Brotherhood bosses are. Organised and violent. I decide to tell him why I'm here.

"I'm looking for a stolen jewel. In the shape of a pendant."

"So?"

"It was stolen from a Sorcerer. The Sorcerer traced it here."

"Then the Sorcerer was mistaken."

"I doubt it. And the Sorcerer would pay well to get it back. It's a family heirloom."

Before Casax can reply, he's interrupted by Karlox, a tough enforcer.

"They're dead," says Karlox.

"Who's dead?"

"The three strangers who wanted to see you. They're still upstairs. But dead."

"Burned?" asks Casax.

"No. Stabbed."

Casax's brow furrows.

"What do you mean, stabbed? No one gets stabbed in here unless I say so."

"They weren't by any chance three men who came here to sell you some stolen jewellery, were they?" I ask.

Casax stares at me.

"Time to leave. Investigator."

Knowing that I'm not going to learn anything more, I turn to go. Casax calls after me. When I turn to face him again, he's got a mocking smile on his face.

"That makes seven, I believe."

"Seven? Seven what?"

"Seven bodies. You want to give me and Karlox here any inside information? We figured we might place a little wager with young Moxalan."

His henchman Karlox laughs like this is a great joke. I try to disguise my feelings, without success. Now word of the betting in the Avenging Axe has reached the Brotherhood. Soon it will be all over Twelve Seas. All over the city, maybe. I'm fast becoming a laughing stock. Damn that idiot Dandelion and her foolish warnings.

I haven't recovered the pendant, though my intuition is telling me pretty strongly that whoever the three guys were, they had it with them. Someone killed them, and made off with it, probably using the fire as a distraction. It was a neat piece of work. It's not easy removing stolen goods from under the noses of the Brotherhood.

It's a relief to get out of the smoky building. Not much relief, though, as the sun hits me full in the face. Despite the commotion caused by the fire, the dwa dealers are still doing a brisk trade in the alleyway.

Three more dead. Seven since I started looking. A bloodbath? Possibly Dandelion was right. Maybe she can read the stars. Maybe she can really talk to the dolphins. I wonder how many bodies Makri is betting on. I'd expect her to go for a high total. She's used to a lot of carnage. As I'm so annoyed at Makri, I'm very tempted to refuse to investigate the accusation of theft against her. Let her sort it out herself. I sigh. If I let her sort it out herself she won't mind at all, but she'll end up on the gallows. Cursing the woman for her foolish academic pretensions, I set off along the dusty road to the College.

The Guild College is sited at the edge of Pashish, a slightly less unpleasant area than Twelve Seas. The streets are still narrow but they're cleaner, and the aqueducts are in good repair. The tenements are less tall and better spaced. Here and there a small park serves as recreation for the families of artisans and lesser merchants. It's the sons of these artisans and lesser merchants who attend the Guild College, some in preparation for careers in the service of the government and a few of them in preparation for the Imperial University.

Makri is, I believe, the only woman to attend the College, gaining entrance only after some anonymous but wealthy woman with a point to prove promoted her case. The College, discovering to their dismay that their written constitution did not actually forbid it, found themselves the unwilling instructors of a mixed-blood ex-gladiator, and to hear Makri tell it they've been trying to get rid of her ever since. Possibly they already would have had Makri and I not done some good work for Deputy Consul Cicerius last year, as a result of which I think he used his influence to enable her continued attendance.

To me it seems like a lot of trouble for nothing. I can't see what good a sound grounding in the arts of philosophy, rhetoric and mathematics is ever going to do her, and as for her ambition to attend the Imperial University, it's never going to happen. For one thing, their constitution does expressly forbid the admittance of women, and for another, if Makri ever walked through their marble portals, the uproar created by Turai's aristocracy would send a shock wave through the Senate. No Senator would want his son in the same class as Makri, with her Orcish blood, barbaric manners and propensity for wielding an axe.

The College is not a grand affair. No grounds, no quad-
rangles with statues. Not even a fountain. It's a dark old
stone building that used to serve as the headquarters of the
Honourable Merchants Association, till the Association grew
wealthy and moved to a better part of town. Its dim corridors
are full of young students carrying scrolls and trying to look
studious. Several elderly men in togas, presumably professors,
stand around looking severe. Though the wearing of a toga is
standard among Turai's upper classes, you don't see many of
them south of the river.

Professor Toarius has a very fine toga, as I discover when I
enter his office. Gaining entry was easier than I expected, the
receptionist outside not being used to repelling large Investigators. The Professor is elderly, grey-haired, aquiline-nosed and
stuffed full of dignity. He's a man of some reputation among
Turai's academics. He's on the board at the Imperial University and it's counted as a great favour from the Consul to
the humble Guild College that the Professor was appointed to
this position. I understand from Makri that Toarius rules the
establishment in a manner which allows no room for debate.
When I stride into his office he looks up from a dusty old
book and frowns.

"Who let you in?" he demands.

"No one."

"If this is some matter regarding your son's education, you
will have to make an appointment."

"I don't have a son. At least not to my knowledge. Although
I did travel the world as a mercenary in my younger days, so
I admit it's not impossible."

The room is crammed full of books and scrolls. As always
when faced with evidence of learning, I'm uncomfortable.

"I'm here about Makri."

The Professor goes rigid in his chair.

"Get out of my office," he demands.

"What evidence do you have against her?"

Professor Toarius rises swiftly and pulls on a bell rope behind him. The clerk hurries in from the office outside.

"Call our security guards," instructs the Professor.

This is worse than I expected. I feel surprised that Toarius is so unwilling to discuss the matter, and even more surprised that this place actually has security guards.

"You can't just expel Makri like this, Professor."

"I already have. It was a mistake to allow her to attend the College, and now that she has committed theft I have no option but to permanently exclude her."

The door opens behind me and two brawny individuals in rough brown tunics hurry into the room. I ignore them.

"You don't get my meaning, Professor. You can't expel Makri because I won't allow it."

This amuses Toarius.

"You won't allow it? And how will you prevent it?"

"By referring the matter to the Senate. Allow me to introduce myself. I'm Thraxas, Tribune of the People."

"Tribune? That post has been extinct for over a century."

"Till recently revived by Deputy Consul Cicerius. And I have the power to prevent any act of exclusion against any citizen of Turai without the matter being debated in the Senate. So before I'm forced to make the matter public, why don't we discuss it?"

"Do you think that the Senate will have the slightest interest in the fate of an Orcish thief?"

Makri isn't actually Orcish. She has one quarter Orcish blood, along with one quarter Elvish. Having grown up in an Orcish slave pit, she hates them. Calling her an Orc is a deadly insult. I can see why she found life under the Professor tough.

"The Senate will have to show an interest. It's the law, and Cicerius is a stickler for the law."

"I am a good deal better acquainted with Deputy Consul Cicerius than you."

The Professor puts down his book. His frown deepens.

"Are you the same Thraxas who was denounced last year in the Senate for your part in the scandal concerning the Elvish cloth which went missing?"

"Yes. But I was later exonerated."

"No doubt," says the Professor drily. "Few guilty men are convicted in this city. And now you claim to be some sort of employee of the government? I have heard nothing about it."

"I've been keeping it quiet. Now, about Makri. What evidence do you have that she stole the money?"

Professor Toarius doesn't want to discuss it. He abruptly orders his men to throw me out. They hesitate.

"I think this man really is a Tribune. I saw him stop an eviction a few months back ... Senator Lodius was with him ..."

The guards stand awkwardly, not quite knowing what to do. They don't want to offend the Professor, but neither do they want to end up being hauled in front of a Senate committee for interfering with official business. Professor Toarius solves the impasse by marching out of the room, muttering about the degeneracy of a city which can allow a man like me to walk around unpunished.

"Is he always like this?" I ask the guards.

"Yes."

"You appreciate I really am a Tribune of the People? You can't throw me out of this place while I'm conducting an investigation."

The guards shrug. I don't get the impression they're that desperate to do the Professor's bidding. Probably he's not the sort of man to inspire loyalty among his menial staff.

"You know Makri?"

The larger of the two guards almost smiles.

"We know her."

"Violent temper," adds his companion.

"Once chased some poor young guy round the building after he made some comment she didn't like. What does she expect? She doesn't exactly cover herself up a lot."

I ask them what they know about the expulsion. They don't know much.

"We weren't involved. All we heard was that some money went missing and she took it. The Professor told us to make sure she didn't get back in the building."

"Did you look into it at all?"

"Why would we?" asks the larger guard. "We're just here to keep the dwa dealers outside from bothering the students. If the Professor expels someone, it's nothing to do with us."

"She probably stole the money," adds the other guard. "I didn't mind the woman, but she is part Orcish. She was bound to start stealing sooner or later."

"Good body, though," adds his friend. "She should stick to being a dancer."

I ask if they know of anyone who might fill me in on a few more details. They suggest Rabaxos.

"It was his money that went missing. Probably find him in the library now. He's a little guy in a shabby tunic. Always got his nose in a scroll. Father owns a fishing boat but I guess being a fisherman isn't good enough for his son. Why are you so bothered about the girl anyway?"

A good question. I leave them without answering it. It's hot and stuffy inside the old building but I've got more on my mind than the uncomfortable weather. I swore I wouldn't use my Tribunate powers again for any reason. Now, thanks to Makri, I've been forced into it. I know what's going to happen now. People are going to appear at my door, asking for help. Once the downtrodden masses learn that I've invoked my powers, they'll all be looking for assistance. Every person in Twelve Seas with some gripe against authority will be demanding action. I'd better strengthen my door-locking spell. I've no intention of spending my life helping the downtrodden masses; I'm downtrodden enough myself.

That's not the worst of it. Deputy Consul Cicerius was furious when I used my powers during the winter, particularly as it was to aid Senator Lodius, head of the opposition party. If I get involved in anything else of a similar nature, Cicerius will be down on me like a bad spell. Once a man gets involved in politics in this city, there's no telling what might happen. Time was when the Tribunes of the People were forever entering into the political fray. More often than not they ended up being assassinated for their troubles, or dragged up in court on trumped-up charges by their opponents. To be a politician in this city you need a lot of backing, and a lot of backing is something I don't have.

When I remember that not only has Makri forced me into using my legal powers, thereby practically ensuring that I'll be run out of town at the earliest opportunity, as well as placing bets on how many corpses I'm liable to run into in the next few days, but she's also received an invitation to Lisutaris's smart party, I start to seethe. Damn the woman. How can I be expected to get along in this city when I have to act as nursemaid to a pointy-eared ex-gladiator who doesn't know how to behave in a civilised society? It wasn't too long ago that she was terrifying the honest citizens of Twelve Seas by talking publicly about her menstruation problems, and if it's not that, it's killing a dwa dealer and bringing the Brotherhood down on my neck, or getting so drunk when we went to the Elvish Isles that she actually threw up over the Crown

Prince's sandals. Much more of this and I'll be taking a fast horse southwards.

By the time I reach the library—another room containing an indecent amount of books and scrolls—I'm in a thoroughly bad mood. I demand to see Rabaxos and, ignoring the multitude of requests for me to keep my voice down, I keep on demanding till eventually a student leads me behind a book stack to a small table where a puny-looking individual with his hair tied back with a cheap piece of ribbon has his nose firmly in a scroll written in the common Elvish tongue. I speak Elvish myself, though I don't go around studying it in libraries.

"I'm here investigating the theft of your money."

He shrinks back in his chair.

"And if you don't tell me exactly what happened, I'll make sure you end up on a prison ship. It'll be a long time before you get to study an Elvish scroll again."

Chapter Six

On my way back to the Avenging Axe, I call in at the local Messengers Guild station, sending a note to Lisu-taris letting her know what's happened. I suggest she try to locate the jewel again and also suggest she uses her consider-able powers of sorcery to find out what the hell is going on. Seven dead bodies is a lot for one pendant that no one is supposed to know about.

The sun is directly overhead and the streets are intolerably hot and dusty. There's little activity save for a bunch of ragged children splashing around in an old fountain that feeds off the local aqueduct. A few more days like this and the water supply is likely to dry up, which will probably lead to a riot. The mood I'm in, I wouldn't mind doing some rioting. I have the grimmest foreboding about what's going to happen now I've used my Tribune's powers. I'll have to send a report to an official at the Senate, and once that's made public, there's no telling what the result will be.

It's clear to me that there was no proper inquiry at the Guild College. According to the young student Rabaxos he'd left the money in his locker for only a few minutes while he went to hand in a paper to one of his tutors. When he returned, the door had been forced open and the money was gone. I checked the lockers. They're little more than wooden boxes with a clasp. Anyone could have forced it in less than a minute. No one saw the theft, but Makri was observed by several students entering and leaving the locker room around the time of the incident. Apart from that, there doesn't seem to be any evidence against her. This doesn't mean the staff at the College were outraged by her expulsion. Nor were the students. They're all pretty much of the same opinion as Professor Toarius: that it was only a matter of time before Makri's Orcish blood came to the fore and she started stealing.

Normally I'd be inclined to agree. Orcs are thieves, cheats and liars. You can't trust an Orc for a second. Even a small amount of Orcish blood makes a person unreliable. Everyone in Turai knows that. Unfortunately, I also know that Makri didn't steal the money, which means I have to find out who did. It's going to be a lot of work over a measly five gurans, and a lot of work for which I'm not going to be paid. I shake my head. As a general rule, I never investigate for free. It creates the wrong impression.

As for Lisutaris's jewel, that case went bad as soon as it started. If the pendant is really the last reliable way of warning Turai against imminent Orcish invasion, it might be time to consider leaving the city. No matter what Lisutaris believes,

someone else obviously knew all about the pendant, probably before it was stolen. You don't get multiple deaths and a burning tavern over any old piece of jewellery.

The fountain's centrepiece is a small statue of St. Quatinius talking to a whale, modelled on one of the numerous exploits of our city's patron. According to the story, the whale was full of religious knowledge. Perhaps signifying this, water pours from the beast's mouth. I shove a few children out the way and take a drink. I eye St. Quatinius.

"You want to help me sort this out?" I ask. He doesn't reply. To the best of my knowledge St. Quatinius has never come to my aid, though as I'm a man who frequently misses prayers, even though the regular saying of prayers is a legal requirement in Turai, I suppose I can't complain.

Back at the Avenging Axe, I grumble to Tanrose about the undignified outbreak of gambling on matters which are not suitable for gambling, namely Thraxas-related deaths. I'm expecting a sympathetic ear from our kindly cook. Unfortunately Tanrose is in a bad mood and brushes aside my complaints. It's very rare for Tanrose to be in a bad mood. Apparently she's been arguing with Gurd over payments for food deliveries. Gurd is at the far end of the bar, looking the other way, but when I take a beer and a plate of stew over to the far corner of the room he abandons his post at the bar and joins me. He's not happy either.

"Never accuse a cook of paying too much for her eggs and flour," I advise him. "It'll always lead to trouble. Makes them think you don't value their cooking."

"It was an argument about nothing," protests Gurd. "Tanrose just yelled at me for no reason. It must be the heat."

There's an awkward moment of silence. We both know that the usual reason for the rare moments of friction between them is Gurd's inability to express his emotions. He was a fine man with a sword or an axe—no one better—but when it comes to telling his cook he's sweet on her he just can't do it.

"You're going to have to say something sometime," I say, uncomfortable as always about this type of conversation. "It's no good just hanging round looking as miserable as a Niojan whore all day then complaining about her bookkeeping when you can't think of anything else to say."

Gurd shakes his head. In the tremendous heat his long grey hair is matted round his shoulders.

"It's not so easy," he mutters, and falls silent.

"Women, they're all crazy," says Parax the shoemaker, a very unwelcome intruder into the conversation.

I tell him to go away.

"And don't start asking for the latest body count."

"We already heard about the last three," says Parax. "Seven so far. Makes my bet on twenty look pretty good."

"Bexanos the ropemaker put a lot of money on twenty to twenty-five," muses Gurd. "You think it might get that high?"

"Gurd, what's got into you? How could you place bets on how many deaths there are going to be?"

"Why not?" says Gurd. "A bet is a bet."

He has a point there.

"There's no pleasing women," says Parax, returning to his original theme. "My wife, no man could live with her."

Parax's wife might be happier if he spent more time actually making shoes and less sitting around in taverns, but I remain silent, not wishing to be drawn into this discussion.

"But we men, what do we do?" continues Parax. "Pander to them. Run around performing their every whim. It's foolish, but that's life."

By this time Gurd is shifting round in his seat very uncomfortably, having no wish to hear his problems aired in public by anyone, particularly a shoemaker notorious for his lack of tact.

"Take Thraxas," says Parax.

I sit up sharply.

"What about Thraxas?" I say.

"Well, where have you just been?"

I narrow my eyes.

"Working."

"Investigating at the Guild College from what I hear. Trying to sort things out for Makri again."

"What do you mean, again?"

"Come on," scoffs Parax. "You're always running round for that woman. You've been doing it ever since she arrived in the city."

I should come back with a crushing rejoinder but the brazen audacity of Parax's words has left me temporarily speechless.

"Don't worry," chuckles the idiotic shoemaker. "Plenty of men have fallen for girls half their age. And she's got a fine figure, even if she does have Orc blood. Good enough to keep you warm in winter, eh, Thraxas?"

Noticing that I am now about to draw my sword and chop Parax's head off, Gurd lays his hand on my arm. I manage to stifle the urge, but only just.

"Parax, you're as dumb as an Orc. Go and bother someone else."

Parax, like the insensitive troublemaker he is, won't let it go.

"So how often do you work for free?"

"Never."

"And how much is Makri paying you to sort out her problems?"

My bad temper gets a lot worse. Makri appears through the front door, cursing the heat. Perspiration makes her short man's tunic stick to her body.

"Have you been to the College?" she asks immediately.

Parax guffaws.

"What's so funny?" says Makri.

"Thraxas," replies Parax, but noticing that I'm again struggling to draw my sword, he backs off, and moves away from our table. Makri pays him no further attention. She's too eager to know what happened at the College.

"Professor Toarius wouldn't speak to me," I tell her. "He seems to hate you. In fact everyone there seems to hate you."

Makri looks crestfallen. I'm pleased.

"But Rabaxos doesn't really think you stole his money. He didn't accuse you of the theft. Professor Toarius just leapt to that conclusion without any evidence as far as I can see. It's odd the Professor is so vehement. He must know he doesn't have enough evidence to stand up to my investigation."

"He dislikes me enough not to care," says Makri.

"Well, don't despair. And don't attack him with an axe. I'll sort it out. And you can still do your examination."

"I can? How?"

"I used my Tribune's powers to stop the expulsion. That means it has to go before the Senate for discussion, which will take weeks. As of now, you're still a student and can take the exam on schedule, in three days' time."

Makri is grateful, though you'd hardly know it. She mumbles a barely discernible thank-you. She's another one who's uncomfortable about showing emotion in public unless driven to it by rage. At the next table, Parax is sniggering. I rise to my feet.

"I have investigating to do," I say, and depart briskly towards the stairs. I've barely sat down at my desk to consider matters when a messenger appears at my door carrying a missive from Lisutaris.

Have extended my powers, the message reads. *Believe that*

jewel has now been transported to Blind Horse tavern in Kushni.
Proceed there immediately.

I shake my head. The Blind Horse in the Kushni quarter. I wouldn't have thought it possible, but the taverns are getting worse. The Blind Horse is the sort of place a man is grateful to come out of alive. If the clientele don't get you, the klee will. With such a dubious venue as my next destination, I attempt to load a couple of spells into my memory. It takes a lot of effort. My sorcerous powers, always slight, are getting weaker every day. I still advertise myself as a Sorcerous Investigator to bring in the public, but really my powers are becoming negligible. Every time a Sorcerer uses a spell he has to relearn it before using it again, and these days I'm finding it very hard work. The door starts shaking from some violent knocking.

I wrench it open angrily. Casax, local Brotherhood boss, strides in without waiting for an invitation. He looks round with distaste at the mess, which, if I remember correctly, he did last time he was here.

"This place is getting worse."

"At least it hasn't burned to the ground."

Casax smiles.

"We saved most of the important things. Now, would you like to tell me why my headquarters was set on fire? It's the sort of thing I should know. Me being the most important crime boss in the area."

"Yeah, I can see it's bad for your image."

"Very bad. So who did it?"

"How would I know?"

Casax's eyes glint.

"Thraxas. I'm asking you in a friendly manner. I'm feeling friendly because you had the presence of mind to remind that useless Sorcerer of mine that he could put out the fire. Otherwise I'd be here with a dozen men. If you want me to come back with a dozen men I will. But I'd rather you just told me what was going on. I hear you went down to the Spiked Mace looking for some jewellery. Next thing four guys were dead and the Guards are questioning you. They let you out and you come to the Mermaid and what do you know, the Mermaid is burning down and inside are three dead men who just happened to be selling stolen jewellery. Which makes me think you're on the trail of some pretty important gems."

Casax takes a seat.

"Is it anything to do with the Orc girl and the Guild College?"

It's unpleasant to learn that Casax knows so much about my movements, but not a surprise. Casax is sharp as an Elf's ear and he has a lot of men working for him. Few things happen in Twelve Seas without Casax learning of it.

"No. Nothing to do with Makri. She's in a dispute over five gurans. Not enough to interest you."

"Probably not. Though five gurans is five gurans."

The sounds of arguing drift in from the street below. The vendors are still in dispute. Casax already knows all about Makri's problems.

"One of my captains has a son at the College. Wants him to get some qualifications and go to the University. You think that's a good idea?"

I shrug.

"Maybe. Better than a life of crime."

"That depends on the criminal. Anyway, suppose the kid goes to the University and ends up in some post at the Palace or the Abode of Justice, taking bribes from Senators? You think that's not a life of crime?"

"Maybe he'll end up a professor. I believe they're still fairly free from corruption."

"No one is free from corruption in Turai. Still, you might

be right. Education, it's a bit of a mystery to me. I started in the business when I was six, running bets for a bookmaker. So I never had much time for school. But if my captain wants to send his son to the College, I'm not against it."

He pauses, temporarily distracted by the increasing vehemence of the argument outside.

"Incidentally, this son I mentioned thinks that the Orc girl didn't take the money."

"She didn't."

"You'll have a hard time proving it, Investigator. Up there Professor Toarius is the only one with authority. The Consul appointed him as a favour to the struggling citizens of Twelve Seas. I doubt he's going to pay much attention to you."

"He might."

"You want that I should use a little influence? Old Toarius will back down quick enough if he finds his staff are about to withdraw their labour. Or maybe not turning up to work at all due to some mysterious warnings."

The Brotherhood could certainly close the College if they wanted to. No porter or delivery man is going to go against an instruction from their guild not to work, and the Brotherhood has great influence in the guilds.

"I'll sort it out. Why would you want to help anyway?"

Casax shrugs.

"Like I said, I don't mind doing you a favour, Investigator. Providing you tell me about the jewel. Who are you trying to recover it for?"

"That would be none of your business."

"Not something I ever like to hear," counters Casax. "Everything in Twelve Seas is my business."

"Nothing I do is your business, Casax. You might have the local guilds in awe of you but you don't scare me. So why don't you take a walk?"

"I'd say if Lisutaris hired you to find a jewel it must be a valuable item. Sorcerous probably."

He knows about Lisutaris. I try not to look surprised.

"I read the message on your desk, Investigator," says Casax. I look foolishly at my desk, where Lisutaris's message to me is lying in plain view. And now Casax has read it. I can't believe I've been so careless. He rises to leave.

"You know, I feel sort of sorry for that Orc girl. Working here all day and all night to pay for her classes. Especially as she's so good with a sword. She ought to work for me. Let me know if you need some help at the College. Be a lot easier than using your Tribune's powers. That's going to get you into big trouble."

Casax departs. I stare at the message on my desk. Thraxas, number one chariot when it comes to investigating, as I've been known to say. But not so good at keeping my business private. I curse. Now the Brotherhood know I'm looking for some important item for Lisutaris, Mistress of the Sky, head of the Sorcerers Guild, there's no telling what's going to happen.

Makri appears in my room without knocking. She asks how things are with the Lisutaris inquiry. I told her most of the details yesterday. A few months ago I realised to my surprise that I now tell Makri most of my business. There's no reason not to, but it breaks a long-term habit of complete privacy.

"It's all getting worse. I'd guess that whoever set this thing in motion hasn't been discreet about it. Either the original thief, or the person who gave him the information, seems to have let half the city know how important that pendant is. Now Casax is on the trail."

"How did he find out?"

"The Brotherhood have spies everywhere."

Makri wonders how many people could know of the pendant.

"Very few, according to Lisutaris. The King, the Consul, the Deputy Consul, maybe a couple of senior Sorcerers. None of them liable to open their mouths, but who knows who else might've got hold of some information and passed it on. All of these people have staff, and staff can be bribed. Lisutaris's secretary knew about the jewel's powers. I'd like to question her but Lisutaris forbids it for some reason."

"She's very protective towards her secretary," says Makri.

"How do you know that?"

"She told me at the Sorcerers Assemblage. While we were sharing a thazis stick. Some sort of young relation, I seem to remember. Niece or something."

"You're getting very intimate with our Chief Sorcerer."

"You know she invited me to her masked ball?" says Makri, brightly.

"Really?"

"What costume should I wear?"

"Why would I want to discuss costumes with you? I'm still angry that you've been placing bets on my work."

"I didn't start it," says Makri. "I just joined in after Moxalan started taking bets. Hey, when I arrived in Turai I didn't even know how to gamble. You encouraged me."

She has a point there.

"I didn't encourage you to gamble on things like this."

"Didn't you tell me that you and Gurd once put a bet on how long it would take your commanding officer to die after he caught the plague?"

"That was different. It was in wartime. And no one liked that commanding officer."

"You're just annoyed because you weren't in on it from the beginning," says Makri, quite shrewdly. "If you'd thought of it first you'd have been sending me out to make anonymous bets on your behalf."

"That's not true. We're talking about my work here. I have a huge responsibility to my clients. How do you think Lisutaris is going to feel if she learns that the degenerates at the Avenging Axe are taking odds on how many people are going to be handing in their togas before the case closes?"

"Moxalan is offering fifty to one for the exact total," says Makri.

"Really? Fifty to one?"

"And twenty to one for a guess to within three of the total."

"I am not interested in any odds," I say, quite sternly.

"Of course not," agrees Makri. "It would be quite unethical. Even though you are a man with plenty of inside information and would have a huge advantage when it comes to placing a bet at the very attractive odds of fifty to one..."

I shake my head.

"No one has ever accused me of unethical behaviour."

"That's just ridiculous," says Makri. "People accuse you of unethical behaviour all the time. No one in Turai gets accused of being unethical more often than you. Just last week—"

"That's quite enough," I say, interrupting before Makri can complete whatever damaging story she has in mind. I change the subject and ask if Gurd and Tanrose are showing any signs of making up.

"No. Still arguing."

It's a worry. If things came to a crisis and Tanrose left the tavern I'd miss her cooking desperately. I'm still reeling from the blow of Minarixa the baker's death last year. Her daughter has taken over the bakery but it's never been the same. Minarixa really understood pastry. It was a rare gift.

Makri looks thoughtful.

"I was champion gladiator. And I taught a puny young Elf

to be a champion fighter. And I'm top of the class in every subject."

"So?"

"So I have natural talents. I've never thought of applying them to other people's problems, but probably if I put my mind to it I could help."

"You do that, Makri."

The thought of Makri as some kind of relationship counsellor makes me shudder. I'm still shuddering as I leave the tavern and make my way past the arguing vendors. If Makri puts her mind to fixing the rift between Gurd and Tanrose, God alone knows what disaster will result.

CHAPTER SEVEN

K ushni, in the centre of the city, is one of the worst parts of town. Bad things happen here. As I'm stepping over the drunken bodies on the pavement I wonder, as I occasionally do, how exactly I ended up being the person who tries to fix the bad things. There are plenty of other ways of making a living. Dandelion sits on the beach and talks to dolphins. She seems to manage okay.

I check my sword is loose in its sheath, allow a scowl to settle on my features—which it does quite easily—and step into the Blind Horse, home to dwa dealers, gamblers, robbers and murderers. Whores with red ribbons in their hair mingle with intoxicated sailors looking for an opportunity to spend the money they risked their lives to earn. At the bar two

Barbarians are arm-wrestling while their companions shout
drunken encouragement. I bump into a man I haven't seen
for five years but used to know quite well.

"Demanius."

"Thraxas."

Demanius is around the same age as me. A lot thinner, and
his hair has gone completely grey. Still a tough-looking character, though. We were in the army together. The last time I
saw him he was working for the Venarius Investigation Agency,
a very respectable organisation, well liked by the authorities.
When I was in Palace Security we'd often find ourselves working alongside Venarius's agents. I ask what brings him to the
Blind Horse.

"I felt like a drink," he replies, not feeling the inclination
to tell me his business.

"So did I."

We make our way to the bar, carefully avoiding the noisy
Barbarians. The air is thick with thazis smoke and the aroma
of burning dwa drifts down from the rooms upstairs. You'd
be surprised who you might find upstairs in a tavern like
this, partaking of illegal narcotics. Members of Turai's upper
classes, not wishing to be found using the substance in their
homes, are not above visiting dubious establishments to feed
their habit.

The Venarius agency has plenty of money. I let Demanius
pay for the beer.

"How's life in Thamlin?" I ask.

The agency headquarters is up close to Thamlin, where the
Senators live.

"Very peaceful. But they keep sending me here."

I'm feeling uneasy. So is Demanius. Meeting another Investigator while out on a case is rare. When it happens I never
know quite what to do. If Demanius is working on the same

case as me it won't do me any good to have him solve it before me. Bad for my reputation and bad for my income. I drink my beer quickly and then tell Demanius that I'm due upstairs for a private appointment.

"As am I," says Demanius.

I'm lying. I don't know if he is. As Investigators go, I wouldn't class Demanius as sharp as an Elf's ear. There again, he's not dumb as an Orc either. If he's here fishing for information he's not getting anything from me. We cross the room, wary of each other, hardly noticing the whores who flop around the tables, or the Barbarians, who are now throwing knives at a target on the wall. The stairs are dark and narrow with a flickering torch providing insufficient light. We're almost at the top when a door opens and a woman emerges. She's wearing the garb of a common market trader and looks out of place. There's a strange expression on her face but when she recognises Demanius she starts to speak.

"The pendant," she says.

I might be getting somewhere at last. She opens her mouth again. Then she falls down dead. So no real progress.

Demanius sprints up the last few stairs. I sprint after him. He bends down to examine the body. There's a great wound in the woman's back, still pumping blood. Demanius draws his sword and charges into the room she came out of. I'm at his heels. Inside we find a man sitting on a chair, staring into space.

Demanius starts barking out questions. I hold up my hand.

"He's trying to speak."

The man's voice comes slowly, from a long way away.

"I'm King of Turai," he says. Then he slumps forward. It's an odd thing to say. Whoever he is, he isn't the King. I feel for the pulse on his neck. There isn't one. He's dead. There are no wounds on his body. Really he looks tolerably healthy. But he's still dead.

I'm becoming very familiar with this scene. More deaths and the pendant still missing. Demanius, lither than me, hauls himself out of the window and drops into the alley below. I don't follow him. Whoever is responsible for this latest outrage is probably long gone. Besides, with my weight I don't fancy the drop. A man doesn't want to break his ankle in this place.

I stare at the body still slumped on the chair, trying to figure out the cause of death. I don't believe it was from natural causes. Doesn't look like poison. Is there sorcery in the air? I look around, trying to sense it. With my own sorcerous background I can usually tell if magic has been used recently, but I can't say for sure. Maybe, faintly.

Outside, a few customers have gathered to look at the dead woman, whose blood still seeps on to the floorboards. They don't appear too interested and no one protests as I quickly search the pocket on her market worker's apron. I find nothing, but I notice a tattoo on her arm. Two clasped hands. The mark of the Society of Friends. The Society is a criminal gang, based in the north of the city. They're bitter rivals with the Brotherhood. Last year there was a murderous war over territory and the feud is still smouldering. Whoever this woman is, I doubt she's the market worker she pretends to be. Or pretended to be.

Someone has finally summoned the landlord. He puffs his way up the stairs with a couple of henchmen, complaining about the inconvenience of always having to carry bodies out of his tavern.

"You could open an establishment in a better part of town," I suggest. "But you'd probably miss the excitement. You know who this woman is?"

"Never seen her before. Who are you?"

"Thraxas. Investigator."

The landlord spits on the floor.

"That's what I think of Investigators."

His henchmen get ready to run me off the premises. I save them the trouble by leaving. There's not a lot of point in sticking around. No one in this place is going to answer questions. I'm not certain I could muster any questions. A peculiar feeling of gloom is settling over me. It's starting to seem like I'm never going to find this pendant. Every time I get close all I find is more dead bodies. A man can only take so many dead bodies, even a man who's used to them.

Walking back through Kushni, I try to review the situation, but I have no real idea what's going on. I'm particularly troubled by the death of the man in the chair. Sword wounds are one thing but a death you can't explain always spells trouble. When I reach Moon and Stars Boulevard I'm uncertain even which way to turn. Should I go back to the Avenging Axe? Possibly I should head north to Truth is Beauty Lane, home of the Sorcerers, and report to Lisutaris. But what's the point? She'll only send me out to some other godforsaken tavern where I'll find a pile of dead bodies.

It's hot as Orcish hell. I've been in cooler deserts. My head hurts. Maybe a beer will help. It often does. I look around for a tavern, somewhere where there's unlikely to be anyone being murdered, at least not until I've had a drink. I've just spotted a reasonable-looking establishment across the road when a carriage pulls up in front of me. An official carriage, with a driver in uniform and the livery of the Imperial Palace. The door opens and a toga-clad figure leans out.

"Thraxas. How fortunate. I was on my way to visit you."

It's Hansius, assistant to Deputy Consul Cicerius. He's a smart, handsome young man, son of a Senator, on his way up the ladder in public life. So far he's doing well. Hasn't been involved in anything scandalous and even stayed sober at the Sorcerers Assemblage, an event notable for its drunkenness and degeneracy.

"Cicerius wants you to visit him right away."

I'm still looking at the inviting tavern across the road.

"Tell him I'm busy."

"It's an official summons."

"I'm still busy."

"Doing what?"

My head hurts more.

"Do I accost you in the street and ask you your business? I'm busy. Tell Cicerius I'll come later."

"If you require beer I am sure the Deputy Consul can provide it," says Hansius, which is perceptive of him.

"The Deputy Consul serves wine, as I recall. And he's miserly with it."

Hansius looks stern.

"Official summons."

I climb into the carriage. We ride slowly north towards the Palace. Our official vehicle has right of way but the streets are so crowded it's still a slow journey. Since our King's diplomacy opened up the southern trade routes a few years ago, commerce in Turai has mushroomed and trade wagons roll in all day. At the corner of the street that leads to Truth is Beauty Lane we're held up for a long time by a huge wagon that's trying to manoeuvre its way round a corner it wasn't designed to turn. The driver curses, and shouts at his four horses.

"Big delivery."

"On its way to Lisutaris's villa, I believe," Hansius informs me. "They're building a theatre in the grounds for the performers to use at the ball."

This worsens my mood. I ask Hansius if he's going. He is, of course.

"I accompany the Deputy Consul to all such events."

Having learned to be tactful as a young man in public service, Hansius doesn't ask me if I'm invited. He knows very well that since being sacked from my job at the Palace I'm not on the guest list for smart parties. To hell with them. Who wants to go to a masked ball anyway? I can just imagine Deputy Consul Cicerius prancing round in a costume. It's unbecoming. I wouldn't offend my dignity.

At the Palace grounds I'm searched for weapons, and before entering the outlying building that houses Cicerius's offices I'm examined by a government Sorcerer, checking to see if I might be carrying any dangerous spells or aggressive sorcerous items.

"You can't see the Deputy Consul while carrying a sleep spell."

I turn to Hansius to protest.

"You expect me to give up my spells? I didn't ask to visit."

There's no use protesting. Palace Security is very sensitive about anyone who isn't a member of the Sorcerers Guild bringing usable spells anywhere near the King. The official Sorcerer holds out a magically charged crystal which I unwillingly take hold of. I feel the sleep spell draining away through my fingers.

"It takes a lot of work to learn these things, you know. Is anyone going to compensate me for my wasted effort?"

Hansius leads me through the marble corridors towards Cicerius's office. Everything here is elegant—pale yellow tiled floors. Elvish tapestries on the walls, each window, no matter how small, decorated with artfully stained glass—and I get a pang of regret for the fine office in a fine building I used to inhabit when I was an investigating Sorcerer at the Palace. The King's residence is one of the finest buildings in the west, full of artwork to rival that of many larger states, and the buildings of his senior officials are likewise well appointed. While I'm not a man who's too concerned with works of art, I can't help feeling a twinge of grief as I realise that everywhere I look there's a bust or statue that would cost more than I'll earn in a year. Even the clerks' desks are made of dark wood imported from the Elvish Isles.

Possibly I shouldn't have got so drunk at my boss Rittius's wedding that I was immediately fired for outraging public decency. But Rittius hated me anyway. He was just looking for an excuse.

My visit to the Deputy Consul's office follows a long-established pattern. Cicerius roundly condemns me for my behaviour and I try vainly to defend myself. Any time I've worked for Cicerius there's come a point when he's felt the need to point out that I'm a disgrace to the fair city of Turai. After a little preparatory sarcasm, he starts laying in with the criticism even though, as I point out, I'm not working for his office at the moment.

"But it was this office which gave you the post of Tribune. On the strict understanding that you were not to go around abusing your powers."

"I wouldn't say I'd been abusing them. Anyway, Professor Toarius abused his first. I had to do something."

Cicerius points a bony finger at me.

"Any use of your Tribunate powers is an abuse. It was merely a device to let you enter the Sorcerers Assemblage. Look what happened when you forbade Praetor Capatius to evict these tenants during the winter."

"You don't have to remind me. The Praetor tried to have me killed."

Cicerius rattles on. As Turai's foremost public orator, he has no trouble inventing new terms of abuse. The Deputy Consul is of the opinion that the prospect of a common man from Twelve Seas getting involved in the politics of our city state is just a step away from complete anarchy.

"Who can say what will happen now?"

I'm not here to argue civil politics with Cicerius, I just want him to get to the point so I can get on with my investigation.

"It was never a good idea that Tribunes could hold up public affairs. Their power of referring matters to the Senate was an anomaly. That is why the post was abolished last century. I must insist that you drop your investigation."

As I suspected from the start, Cicerius shows no sign of providing me with beer. With the heat, my aching head and the intolerable sound of Cicerius lecturing me, I'm coming close to breaking point, a point at which I shall roundly abuse the Deputy, march out of the house and thereby do great damage to my career. I interrupt the flow to tell him that much as I didn't want to use my Tribunate powers, I couldn't see a ready alternative.

"And as I recall, Deputy Consul, you ran for the election largely on an honesty ticket. Cicerius never takes a bribe and he never prosecutes an innocent man, so they say. Everyone's still impressed by the way you've defended people in court because you believed them to be innocent, even when it meant going against your party."

This gets his attention. Cicerius never minds hearing good things said about himself.

"So consider things from my point of view. Or, more to the point, from Makri's. She's completely innocent of the theft. You shouldn't find that too hard to believe because you've met her and you know what she's like. Demented but honest. And you also know how hard she works for these examinations. All the while slaving away as a barmaid to support herself and pay for her classes, which don't come cheap. I thought that would impress you in particular."

Cicerius purses his thin lips. He takes my meaning. Though born into the aristocratic class, Cicerius wasn't born rich. His father died when he was an infant, leaving a family in poverty because he'd invested all his money in a fleet of trading ships which went down in a storm. There was a dispute over the insurance and Cicerius's mother, outsmarted by her late husband's business partners, ended up in penury. This meant that Cicerius himself had to work extremely hard to make his way through university and up the ranks of government. Though he's a rich man now, his younger years were one long struggle.

The reason I know all this, the reason everyone knows all this, is that Cicerius himself has not been above bringing his background up on any occasion he needs to remind the Senate that he's a self-made man, and proud of it.

"Are you going to let a citizen of Turai—"

"Makri is not a citizen of Turai. Makri is an alien with Orcish blood."

"Who did a good job for you when you needed someone to look after that Orcish charioteer last year. Are you going to let a hard-working young woman be denied her chance to sit her examination because Professor Toarius has taken an irrational dislike to her? And please don't tell me that Consul Kalius has done the poor a great favour by appointing Toarius as head of the Guild College."

"Consul Kalius has done the poor a great favour by appointing Toarius as head of the Guild College," says Cicerius.

"I don't care. He's not stopping Makri from taking the examination. I've forbidden her expulsion. It can't go ahead before it's been discussed by a Senate committee, and by that time I'll have evidence to prove her innocence. And nothing you can say can change my mind. I'm offended that a champion of justice like yourself should be ranged against me."

Cicerius is almost at a loss for words. I've managed to flummox the great orator, if only because he's honest at heart. An appeal to justice wouldn't have gotten me very far with any other official in this city. The Deputy Consul fixes me with a piercing lawyer's stare.

"You seem extremely concerned for the welfare of this young woman. Is there some arrangement between you?"

I'm staggered that the Deputy Consul could suggest such a thing.

"If I prove her innocence she won't slaughter everyone at the College. I guess you could call that an arrangement."

Cicerius isn't happy but really he's in an impossible situation. He can't bring himself to connive in a blatant injustice, and even if he could, there is no legal way to rescind my Tribune's decree. Only I can do that, and I've made it clear I'm not going to.

"Very well," he says. "You may continue with your investigation. And when the matter comes to the Senate committee I will ensure that it is looked into thoroughly. But I warn you, if there are any political repercussions of your actions, if Senator Lodius and his opposition party again manage to make you their tool in an action against the government, I will personally rescind your Investigator's licence. With your past record, it will be quite in order for me to do so."

Having nothing more to say, I make to leave.

"One moment," says Cicerius. "Why did Lisutaris, Mistress of the Sky, visit you?"

"Why do you ask?"

"Lisutaris is head of the Sorcerers Guild and an important

person in the interests of this city state. If she is in any sort
of trouble I would naturally wish to know."

"If she was in any trouble and she'd consulted me, I doubt
I'd tell you. I respect my clients' privacy. But she didn't come
to see me, she came to see Makri."

"Really?"

"Yes. She was inviting her to her ball."

Cicerius is surprised. Twenty years ago, a woman like Makri
would never have been allowed to attend such an event.

"So be careful who you bump into on the night. If it's a
crazy-looking woman with an axe, don't ask her about college."

I depart, leaving Cicerius displeased with the laxity of manners in modern-day Turai. As a Sorcerer mutters a spell to let
me out of the building, I'm wondering what sort of costume
our Deputy Consul will be sporting at the ball. I just can't
imagine him in fancy dress.

CHAPTER EIGHT

Back in Twelve Seas, I take the short cut through St. Rominius's Lane, not caring if the dark alley might be filled with dwa dealers. If they bother me they'll regret it. I don't see any dwa dealers but I do see a unicorn. I stand and stare in amazement. You don't find unicorns in Turai. You find them mainly in the magic space, which can only be visited by sorcery. As for the real world, unicorns only appear in a very few places, each of these places being of some mystical significance. The fairy glade, for instance, deep in the forests that separate Turai from the wastelands, has its share of the one-horned animals, and there's reputed to be a colony way out in the furthest west. Other than that, you'd have to go to some of the remoter Elvish Isles to see one. Wherever you might expect to find a unicorn, it wouldn't be in a noisy, busy, dirty city like Turai. Absolute anathema to the refined breed.

Yet here it is, snowy-white, golden-horned, standing in a grimy little alleyway looking at me like it hasn't a care in the world. Faced with the fabulous creature, the thought quickly flashes across my mind that if I could capture it, I might be able to sell it for a healthy profit to the King's zoo. He's been short of fabulous creatures since his dragon was chopped up a year or two back.

"Nice unicorn," I say, holding out my hand in a reassuring manner and stepping forward carefully. As soon as I move, the unicorn turns and bolts round the corner. I fly after it but it's vanished.

"Stupid beast," I mutter, and hurry on. Now it will have plunged into Quintessence Street, where it will be apprehended and sold for profit by some person far less needy than me. If I get there quickly I still might be up for a share.

I rush down the alley, oblivious to the heat and dust, and burst into the main street, eagerly looking in every direction at once.

"It's mine, I saw it first, you dogs!" I cry, and brandish my sword to discourage anyone from muscling in on the deal.

Two women at a watermelon stall look at me, puzzled.

"What's yours?" they ask.

"The unicorn. Which way did it go?"

The women burst out laughing, and keep laughing for a long time. It is apparently the funniest thing they've ever heard. And yet I'm right next to the mouth of the alley. It had to have emerged here. I confront the watermelon sellers.

"Didn't a unicorn come out of that alleyway?"

They look at me with what might be pity.

"Dwa," says one.

"A serious addiction," agrees her friend.

I look round wildly. Apart from a few people staring at the mad person shouting about unicorns, no one in Quintessence Street is showing signs of abnormal activity. It's quite obvious that no single-horned fabulous creature has featured here recently. So it just ran round the corner and vanished from sight.

I realise that someone has been playing a trick on me. A Sorcerer's apprentice with nothing better to do, most probably. He'll regret it if I catch hold of him.

"Okay, I'll take a watermelon then," I say to the women.

I eat it on the street, cooling down from my exertion. What was I thinking, chasing after an obvious illusion? I must be getting foolish. Flocks of stals—unfortunately real—are perched listlessly on the roofs. These small black scavenging birds spend their time picking up scraps from the market, but in the deadening heat even they're finding it tough to make a living.

Makri is waiting for me in my office. I'm not mentioning the unicorn to her.

"You know I have to stand up and talk to the whole class?"

"I believe you mentioned it."

"I have to walk out in front of everyone and declaim in public."

"So you said."

"It's worse now. I have to stand up and talk to a class of people who all think I'm a thief! Is that fair?"

When Makri is in a bad mood her hand has a tendency to stray towards where her sword would be, if she was wearing one. She's doing it now, but is clad only in her chainmail bikini, without weapons. In the sweltering heat sweat pours down her body. I'm given to believe that the lower-class elements in Twelve Seas like the effect.

"Have you proved me innocent yet? No? Why not?"

"I've been busy."

"Will it take long?"

"I'm involved in a very important case, Makri. Vital for the city. With bodies everywhere."

"How many bodies?"

"Nine."

Makri purses her lips.

"I've bet on fourteen. Do you think I should up it?"

"Don't talk to me about that."

She shrugs.

"So don't I matter as much as this other case?"

"No," I say.

"Why not?"

"Because the other case involves a matter of national importance!" I explode. "And also I'm being paid."

"Fine," retorts Makri. "Of course when I was saving your neck last winter from that man with the magic sword I didn't stop to ask if I was being paid or not. I just saved your life. I didn't wait around to check on any possible remuneration, just weighed in there and risked my own life to save yours. But hey, I'm only a barbaric gladiator. When I was growing up I didn't learn all the rules of civilised society. I just did what I thought was the right—"

"Makri, will you shut the hell up!"

When Makri arrived in Turai I swear she wasn't capable of these sustained bursts of withering eloquence. I blame the rhetoric classes.

"I'll sort it out for you. And meanwhile you can still take the examination."

"In front of people who think I'm a thief."

I ask Makri what she's doing in my office when she should be working downstairs. She looks uncomfortable.

"Gurd and Tanrose are still arguing. The atmosphere's bad."

I'm still curious as to why she's in my office instead of her own room.

"Dandelion's there. I said she could stay a while."

"Why do you put up with that woman? Sling her out."

Makri shrugs, and when I press the point she becomes agitated. I drop it. Makri has to return to her work anyway so I accompany her downstairs. I should send another message to Lisutaris letting her know what happened at the Blind Horse. I'll do it after a beer or two.

At the bar I'm accosted by Parax the shoemaker, who, in keeping with his normal practice, is not making shoes at this precise moment. He asks me how my day has been.

"Bad."

"Any dead bodies lying around?"

"Since when would you care, Parax?"

"Can't a man worry about his friends?"

It's news to me that Parax is my friend. Telling him that he can look elsewhere for his inside information, I take a beer, a bowl of venison stew, a plate of yams and a large apple pie to a table, where I read the latest copy of *The Renowned and Truthful Chronicle of All the World's Events*, one of Turai's news sheets, and a fertile source of information on the city's many scandalous occurrences.

There doesn't seem to be much scandal today apart from a report that Prince Frisen Akan, heir to the throne, has extended his holiday at his country retreat, which, as everybody knows, is a coded way of saying that the King has sent him out of town in an effort to get him sober. The Prince is degenerate even by royal standards. At one time it would have been a better-kept secret, but these days, with Senator Lodius's opposition party grown so powerful, fewer people are feeling it necessary to revere the royal family. When I was a boy no one would have dared speak a word against the King, but these days you can hear talk in many quarters about how we might be better off as a democracy. Certain other members of the League of City States have already been riven by civil war as the power of their kings waned. If Senator Lodius and his Populares party get their way, it'll happen in Turai sooner rather than later.

Gurd sits down heavily beside me.

"I can't take any more of this," he confides. "That fishmonger was here again today and Tanrose was all over him."

"Gurd, you're exaggerating."

"Does it take two hours to order fish for next week's menu? It's not that popular an item."

"I don't know. A lot of dockers like it."

"I'd say dockers usually go for stew," says Makri, appearing next to our table with a tray of drinks in her hand.

"No, I think they still prefer fish."

"How would you know?" demands Makri. "It's me that takes the orders."

"I'm an Investigator. I notice things."

"Tanrose didn't have to—" begins Gurd.

"There's definitely more stew sold to dockers than fish," states Makri emphatically.

"I beg to differ. Fish is still the staple diet of the dockers in Twelve Seas."

"How can you say that, Thraxas? It's just not true. No wonder you're always having trouble solving your cases if you can't observe a simple thing like who eats—"

"Enough of this!" yells Gurd, banging his fist on the table.

"Is Tanrose still upset at you?" asks Makri.

"Yes. No. Yes. I don't want to discuss it."

Seeing my old companion-in-arms looking as miserable as a Niojan whore, I wish there was something I could do to help.

"Maybe it's time for some action," I suggest. "Remember when we spent five days in that mountain fort waiting for the Simnians to attack? And eventually Commander Mursius said he'd be damned if he was going to wait any more than five days for a Simnian and he led us out and we drove the Simnians way back over the border?"

"I remember," says Gurd. "What about it?"

"Well maybe it's time you asked Tanrose to marry you."

There's a slight pause.

"Did I miss something?" says Makri.

"I don't think so."

"Well how did you get from attacking the Simnians to Gurd asking Tanrose to marry him?"

"It's obvious. There comes a time when it's no good sheltering behind the walls any longer. You have to attack. Or, in this case, get married."

Makri considers this.

"What if the Simnians had brought up reinforcements?"

"We'd have beaten them as well."

"What if they'd made an alliance with the Orcs and had some dragons lying in wait?"

"Very unlikely, Makri. The Simnians have never been friends with the Orcs."

"So you're saying I should ask Tanrose to get married?" says Gurd, looking quite troubled at the thought.

"Maybe. But you know I've always been useless with women."

Makri nods her head.

"Tanrose tells me you treated your wife really badly."

"Tanrose should keep her mouth shut."

Gurd looks offended.

"About certain subjects only," I add.

"That fishmonger has always been in pursuit of Tanrose. I'm banning him from the tavern from now on."

"Most people prefer stew anyway," says Makri. "And Thraxas eats enough of it to keep you in business."

But by now Gurd has raised his brawny figure and departed, looking thoughtful. Makri takes his seat.

"Why have you always been so bad with women?" she asks.

I shrug.

"Don't know. Just never learned what to do, I suppose."

"I thought maybe it might be because you drink too much."

"Yes, also I drink too much. But at least I don't take dwa."

Four dock workers, waiting for the drinks presently marooned on Makri's tray, call loudly for their beer. Makri ignores them.

"I don't take dwa. Well, not for a while. Don't start criticising me. I'm not the one who's useless at relationships."

Makri is useless at relationships. She spent all last winter snivelling about some Elf she met on Avula because he didn't keep in touch with her. I don't bother to point this out. The dockers call for their beer. Makri curses them loudly and tells them to wait.

The front door opens and Lisutaris, Mistress of the Sky, strides majestically into the tavern. This time, she hasn't bothered to disguise herself.

"We need to talk," she says, and heads for the stairs.

"Thanks for the invitation," says Makri, but Lisutaris doesn't acknowledge her, obviously having more important things on her mind than social functions. I follow Lisutaris upstairs while Makri takes her tray of beer to the thirsty dockers. As I'm climbing the stairs I can hear them arguing. It's a while since Makri punched a customer but she seems to be working up to it again.

In her full costume Lisutaris stands out strikingly in my shabby office. Her official Sorcerer's rainbow cloak positively vibrates with colour. Unusually for her she doesn't take a seat but paces up and down nervously, lighted thazis stick in hand.

"Things taken a turn for the worse?" I enquire.

"They have. Consul Kalius suspects that the pendant is missing. He sent his representative to my villa this morning specifically to ask if it was still secure in my hands."

"How did the Consul learn of the affair?"

Lisutaris glares at me.

"How? I thought it might have something to do with you barging your way all over town leaving a trail of dead bodies in your wake. I appreciate you're not famous for your subtlety, but when I hired you I wasn't expecting you to start slaughtering the city's inhabitants. It was bound to cause comment eventually."

I'm astonished by the effrontery of the woman.

"I haven't killed anyone. The way people have been after this pendant it's no wonder the Consul's got wind of it. I can't believe you'd blame me."

"You can't? Why not? You're supposed to be an Investigator. And yet on the simplest of cases you have notably failed to produce any results. Tell me, Thraxas, on most of your cases do you have exact information as to the whereabouts of the stolen item?"

"No."

"Yet I have three times told you precisely where the pendant could be located and on each occasion you have failed to retrieve it. Instead, all I get is messages telling me that some brutal slaughter has occurred and the gem is missing again. Don't you think it would be a good idea to arrive in time to locate the item I'm paying you to find?"

Lisutaris halts in the middle of the room and fixes me with a hostile stare. Coming from the head of the Sorcerers Guild, this is quite disconcerting. Lisutaris is one of the most powerful magic users in the world and if she decided it was time to use a little magic on an errant Investigator I wouldn't want to be that Investigator. I'm wearing a fine spell protection necklace but no such item could hold out against the might of Lisutaris for long.

That being said, I don't allow anyone to enter my room and abuse me. I meet her gaze and inform her coldly that if I'm not given enough time to do the job then the job won't get done, and besides, it would be a help if she'd told me the full facts of the case.

"Are you implying I have withheld information?"

"Most clients do. You said that no one knew the power of this pendant. That's obviously not true. From the way people have been killing each other to get hold of it, I'd say its importance was well known to someone. When you first arrived here the job looked simple and we were in a hurry so I didn't get the full background to the case. Maybe I should have. Who else in your immediate circle knew you had the pendant, for instance?"

"No one but my secretary."

"Then maybe we should have a few words with your secretary."

"You will not investigate her," says Lisutaris, quite emphatically.

"I think I should."

"I am not interested in what you think. You will not speak to my secretary and that is final. If knowledge of the pendant's true significance has somehow been learned, it is unfortunate but no longer relevant. I don't care how it came to happen; the point is I must have the pendant back immediately. Do you realise that Consul Kalius will be at my house in two days' time? He is suspicious already. He's bound to ask to see the pendant."

"Couldn't you fob him off with an imitation?"

"If it were only the Consul, yes. But he will have with him Sorcerers from the government, all of whom I have invited to my masked ball. No imitation jewel I could fabricate would fool Old Hasius the Brilliant. Hasius is still seething with jealousy over my election as head of the Guild. He'd take one look at an imitation pendant and squawk so loud they'd hear him in Simnia."

Lisutaris finishes her thazis stick and lights another.

"This is such a mess! Damn it, I never wanted to be head of the Sorcerers Guild in the first place. I never asked to be placed in charge of items vital for the defence of the city. The Consul's going to be down on me like a bad spell when he learns I've lost the pendant. Only last month he was telling me that some Orcish prince or other had just conquered a neighbouring country and was looking to set himself up as war leader."

"Prince Amrag?"

Lisutaris nods. Already in the west we've heard quite a few reports about this prince. The Orcs hate us as much as we hate them but they're often more riven by internal warfare than we are, which prevents them from mounting a concentrated attack on us. But every now and then a leader comes along capable of unifying the Orc nations, and when that happens it's but a short step to an invasion of the Human lands. Prince Amrag looks like he might be the Orc to do it, and it might not be too far in the future.

"Maybe it's time to call in someone else."

"What do you mean?" demands Lisutaris.

"If this is so important for Turai, maybe Palace Security should be involved. They could put their whole resources to searching the city."

"Absolutely not," says Lisutaris, shaking her head and lighting another thazis stick. Lisutaris's substantial use of thazis often sends her into a happy dream world, and it's a sign of how deep the crisis is that she shows no signs of relaxing, no matter how many sticks she smokes.

"I cannot own up to the loss of the pendant. I'd be ruined. The King would expel me from the city in disgrace and I'd be shunned in every nation. My family has been in the leading tier of Turanian society for as long as the city's been here, and I refuse to end up a mad old hermit in the wastelands casting horoscopes for travellers."

I break open a new bottle of klee. Lisutaris, not a great drinker, downs a glass in the blink of an eye and holds out her glass for more. I pour her another glass and ask her if she knows of any reason why an operative from the Venarius Investigation Agency might also be on the trail of the pendant.

"I've no idea. Surely it's not possible."

"I'm pretty certain that's what Demanius was doing in the Blind Horse. Before the woman died she seemed to recognise him, and she mentioned the jewel."

"This is a disaster," says the Sorcerer, and starts pacing again.

"It is. So far this pendant has been in the hands of various unknown thieves, the Brotherhood, and the Society of Friends. Both these organisations have contacts all over the city, extending right up into the government. When you add in the fact that whoever stole it in the first place probably knew exactly what they were getting, and probably tried to sell it to someone who also knew all about it, it's pretty clear that the matter is no longer much of a secret. In fact, we might as well assume that everyone knows about it. Are you sure you don't want to call in some outside help?"

Lisutaris doesn't.

"The moment I admit the loss, I'm ruined. We have two days left. You must find the pendant."

"I'll do my best. I'll do better if you fill me in on a few missing details."

"Like what?"

"Like why so many people are dying. It's not credible that they all just happened to kill each other in a fight over the jewel. Thieves don't suddenly kill each other. If one is dominant the others back down after the first sign of violence. None of these crime scenes looked like the scenes I'm used to. It looked to me like something had affected the people in a way that drove them insane. Which would be backed up by some of their dying words. One man told me he was on a beautiful golden ship and another one thought he was King of Turai. Any particular reason why they might be thinking that?"

"Yes," says Lisutaris. "Looking into the green jewel would drive an untrained mind insane. Four people who had all looked into it would be quite likely to kill each other as their dreams took over their reality."

"You're telling me this now? Don't you think you could have mentioned it earlier?"

"I did say that it was a dangerous object," protests Lisutaris.

"Not so dangerous that it was going to lead to such slaughter. So it's quite likely that every time someone gets hold of this pendant they'll go mad, kill their companions and make off with it?"

"Yes. But they won't get far. If they look into it they will probably die even without violence being inflicted on them. It will just break their minds."

I could protest more. Lisutaris really should have given me more information when she hired me. There's not much point in complaining now, though. I'm stuck with it.

"So we now have two problems. One, lots of people seem to know about the jewel. Two, it's going to drive them all homicidally insane."

Lisutaris studies her glass.

"This klee is disgusting. My throat is burning. Where do you buy it?"

"It's supplied to Gurd by a monastery in the hills. The monks distil it in their spare time."

"Do they have a grudge against the city?"

"I find it bracing."

Lisutaris drains her glass and winces again as the fiery spirit trickles down her throat.

"It's poisonous. This liquid would kill you."

She holds out her glass.

"Give me more."

I fill her glass.

"I could ask Gurd to send you a few bottles for your masked ball."

"I don't think the Senators could take it," replies Lisutaris, completely failing to catch my hint that she ought to be inviting me. Not that I really want to go. The sight of Turai's aristocracy disporting themselves in costume is not one that appeals to me. But it still rankles that Makri has an invitation. All she did for Lisutaris at the Assemblage was walk around behind her pretending to be a bodyguard, meanwhile getting so wrecked on thazis, dwa and klee that I had to carry the pair of them home in a carriage. It was me who did all the hard work and her ingratitude is simply appalling. I realise that Lisutaris has been talking to me for some time.

"What were you saying?"

"Have you not been listening?"

"I was contemplating some aspects of the case. Tell me again."

"I can no longer locate the pendant."

"Why not?"

Lisutaris is frustrated at having to repeat herself. Apparently after I failed to find the gem in the Blind Horse she repeated her sorcerous procedure for tracing the pendant but was this time unsuccessful. Someone has now succeeded in hiding the jewel from sorcerous enquiry, no mean feat against the power of Lisutaris. It might mean that it is now in the hands of someone capable of providing some heavyweight sorcerous protection themselves.

"There aren't too many rogue Sorcerers around who could do that. There's Glixius Dragon Killer of course, he might have the power. I haven't seen him for a while but he's been on my mind ever since I saw that woman's Society of Friends tattoo. He used to work with them."

Another possibility is that whoever now has the jewel has wrapped it in red Elvish cloth, which would have the effect of casting an impenetrable shield over the object. No sorcerous enquiry can penetrate the cloth. However, red Elvish cloth is fabulously expensive and very hard to come by. It's illegal for anyone but the King and his ministers to own it.

"Which isn't to say that someone else in the city might have got their hands on some. Another possibility is that the pendant might have left the city. It might be on its way east right now."

Lisutaris looks alarmed.

"Surely no one would be so base as to sell such an item to the Orcs?"

"You'd be surprised how base some people in this city can be."

"You may be right. But not much time elapsed between when the pendant last went missing and the time of my enquiry. I think I'd have picked up the traces were it close to the city. I think it most likely that it is still in Turai, concealed in some manner. Where do you suggest we look?"

"I've no idea. It could be anywhere. If you can't locate it with sorcery, I'm stuck."

"I thought you were an Investigator," says Lisutaris, drily.

"Number one chariot in the field of investigation. But we don't know who took it and Turai's a large city. I'll start making enquiries but it'll take time."

Lisutaris clenches her fists.

"I have no time."

There's a knocking at the door. I open it. Sarin the Merciless is standing outside. Sarin is one of the deadliest killers I've ever met. She has a loaded crossbow in her hand. She points it at my heart.

"Give me the pendant or I'll kill you."

Chapter Nine

"You keep getting in my way," says Sarin.

Sarin the Merciless is as cold as an Orc's heart. Not a woman you can take lightly. She learned her fighting skills from warrior monks and is as ruthless a killer as I've come across in all my years of investigating.

"You know it's illegal to carry a weapon like that inside the city walls?"

"Is that so?"

"It is. But don't get the impression I'm not pleased you visited, Sarin. There are enough warrants out for you for murder and robbery to make a man wealthy."

"Only if he was alive to collect the reward."

Sarin is rather tall. She wears a man's tunic—unusual

enough—and, uniquely for a woman in this city, has her hair cut very short. This is next door to taboo and quite unheard of in civilised society. For some reason I've never been able to fathom, she wears an extraordinary number of earrings, an odd indulgence for a woman whose image is otherwise so severe. She's added a few since I last saw her and the piercings now travel the full semicircle of each ear.

She looks at Lisutaris, meanwhile keeping the crossbow pointed at my chest. A bolt at this range would pin me to the wall. Sarin once shot Makri and it took the power of a magical healing stone to save her life. Round about the same time she killed Tas of the Eastern Lightning, one of Turai's most powerful Sorcerers.

"Who are you?" she demands.

"Lisutaris, Mistress of the Sky," replies the Sorcerer coldly. "Put that crossbow down."

Showing no wish to put the crossbow down, Sarin points it instead at Lisutaris, which is a mistake. Lisutaris makes a slight movement of her hand and the weapon flies from Sarin's grasp to clatter on the floor, ending up under the sink. If Sarin is perturbed she doesn't show it. She steps forward so her face is only a few inches from that of Lisutaris.

"I don't like Sorcerers," she says.

"I don't like you," counters Lisutaris.

Lisutaris is not a woman you can intimidate easily. She fought heroically in the last war against the Orcs, bringing down war dragons from the sky and blasting Orcish squadrons with powerful destructive spells. When her considerable supply of sorcery eventually ran out, she picked up a sword and hewed at the Orcish invaders as their heads appeared over the city walls. I know because I was beside her at the time.

"You might believe that the spell protection charm I

sense on your person will protect you against me. You are mistaken. Remove your face from mine or I will engulf you in flames."

"Will you?" says Sarin, not removing her face. "Before you wore down my protection spell I'd break your neck."

As a sporting man, I wouldn't mind seeing Sarin and Lisutaris squaring off against each other, but it would probably mean my rooms getting wrecked, and when that happens Gurd is never happy about it. So I interrupt.

"Did you come here just to pick fights with my guests? That's something I can usually do myself."

Sarin draws back a few inches.

"No, Thraxas, I came here looking for a pendant. I thought you might have it. Not an unreasonable assumption, given that you were seen at the green jewel's last known location. Do you have it?"

"I don't know what you're talking about."

"The pendant. For far-seeing. Lisutaris hired you to retrieve it for her. Just as I hired men to retrieve it for me. My men ended up dead. I see you fared better."

"I'm a hard man to kill."

An expression of withering contempt flickers over Sarin's features. Not feigned contempt, but real.

"Hard to kill? I've passed by you drunk in the gutter, Thraxas. I could have gutted you had I wished."

"When was this exactly?"

"On one of the many occasions I've been in this city, unde-tected. There are plenty of unsolved crimes which could be laid at my door, Investigator. Some of them investigated by you, without result. The few successes you brag about are as nothing compared to your multitudinous failures."

I don't believe her. Sarin is just angry at me because I've thwarted her in the past. But I notice Lisutaris is looking at me with a new lack of respect. No client likes to hear their Investigator being mocked by a criminal.

"Me lying drunk in the gutter notwithstanding, Lisutaris hasn't lost any pendants that I know about. The Mistress of the Sky merely called in to invite me to a masked ball she's holding in a couple of days. And I'm very gratified to receive the invitation, Lisutaris. I shall be delighted to attend."

"Stop this buffoonery," says Sarin, loudly. She studies my face.

"You don't have the pendant," she says.

She turns her head to Lisutaris and regards her for a few seconds.

"And neither do you."

"So you can read minds?" I ask, intending it to be sarcastic.

"Not exactly," replies Sarin, taking my statement at face value. "But I trained with warrior monks. I can read emotions."

She picks up her crossbow.

"A puzzle," she says, softly. "I knew that the pendant had been intercepted by the Society of Friends. I intended to take it from their operative at the Blind Horse. But someone beat me to it. I thought it might have been you but apparently I was wrong. No matter. I do not doubt that I can find it again. If you get in my way I'll kill you."

Sarin the Merciless departs, closing the door quietly behind her.

"At least we're not the only ones who don't know where the pendant is."

"That is little comfort," says Lisutaris. "Who was that woman?"

"Sarin the Merciless. Ruthless killer. She almost killed Makri and she did kill Tas of the Eastern Lightning though it could never be proved against her. She once blackmailed the Consul's office and made off with enough gold to last her a lifetime, but it hasn't induced her to retire from crime. I get the impression she enjoys it. Of course, she's mentally unwell. That whole part about seeing me lying drunk in the gutter was obviously a hallucination."

"Obviously. Who are her associates?"

"She has no fixed alliances. Did work with Glixius Dragon Killer and the Society of Friends one time, but they fell out, as I recall. She was all set to rob the Society but someone beat her to it."

"Might we use her as a means of finding the pendant?"

"Perhaps. Can you follow her?"

"I can," says Lisutaris. "I will trace her movements round the city and keep you informed. Meanwhile I must urge you to spare no effort in your own search. I must depart now. I'm due at a meeting of Turai's ministers of state."

I speak some words of caution to Lisutaris.

"Sarin is a very dangerous woman. If she can't find the pendant herself she might just decide to search for it at your villa. Perhaps I really should come to the ball."

"Do not trouble yourself," says Lisutaris. "I have adequate security."

She departs. I march straight downstairs for a beer.

"Good meeting?" asks Makri, at the bar.

"Stop talking and give me a beer."

"So what are you as miserable as a Niojan whore about?"

"Nothing."

"Nothing?"

"That's right, nothing. Also, Sarin the Merciless just paid a visit."

Makri is agitated. Sarin once put a crossbow bolt in her chest and Makri would like the opportunity to return the favour.

"I think Sarin must be the only person ever to wound me that I haven't killed in return."

I tell Makri she'll probably get her chance.

"Sarin has a way of appearing when she's not wanted."

"Does this mean you can't investigate at the Guild College?"

"It might have to wait a while."

"It can't wait," insists Makri. "If you don't find the thief soon I'm going to have to do the examination with everyone thinking I'm a criminal."

"Well you'll just have to make the best of it."

"Make the best of it?" says Makri, flushing. "Make the best of it? Is that your advice? I didn't ask you to get involved in the first place. I was quite happy to go up there and kill Professor Toarius. You persuaded me not to and now you're saying I just have to make the best of it?"

Seeing Makri getting angry, the drinkers around us draw back nervously.

"That's right, you'll just have to make the best of it. Just because Lisutaris invited you to her smart party doesn't mean the whole city has to start jumping around for your convenience."

"Aha!" yells Makri. "So that's why you've been acting like a troll with toothache. You're jealous because you can't go to the ball."

"I am not jealous."

"Just like the Elvish princess in the story," says Makri.

"What story?"

"'The Elvish Princess Who Couldn't Go to the Ball.'"

"There's no such story."

"Yes there is. I translated it last year."

I glare at Makri with loathing.

"Fascinating, Makri. I'm gratified to learn that while I'm struggling round the streets fighting criminals you're safe in a classroom translating Elvish fairy stories."

Makri takes her sword from behind the bar.

"I'm off to kill Professor Toarius," she mutters.

I move swiftly to cut off her exit.

"Fine. I'll go investigate at the College."

I grab a bag of food from Tanrose and eat on the hoof. Possibly Makri was right. I should be paying more attention to her problem. It's just that with bodies everywhere, Lisutaris's case was hard to ignore. Till the Sorcerer sends me another lead, however, I've got a little time to investigate the theft. I can't help resenting all the work I'm having to do over a lousy five gurans.

I still have some students left to visit, people who were close to the scene of the crime on the day in question. I set about tracking them down. It takes a lot of trudging round the streets and a lot of knocking at doors where no one is pleased to see me. I work my way northwards through the city, and as the houses become smarter the replies get briefer. Several families flatly refuse to let me in and succumb eventually only to the threat of a court order from the Tribune's Office. There isn't actually a Tribune's Office, but they're not to know that.

"When I heard that the Deputy Consul had reinstated the post of Tribune I did not realise it would lead to the harassment of honest people going about their work," says one angry master glassmaker, upset at me interrupting the family dinner to question his son.

"Just a few questions and I'll be on my way."

This is the eighth house I've visited, so far with no results. For students who are supposed to be learning, the young men at the Guild College seem peculiarly unobservant. I can understand that, I suppose. I studied as a Sorcerer's apprentice for almost a year, and at the end of it all I could remember was the way to the nearest tavern.

I'm shown into an elegant front room which is sufficiently well furnished to make me think that a master glassmaker can't be that bad a thing to be. I wait a long time, and no one offers me a drink; bad manners towards a guest. Even the Consul would offer me wine, and he's never pleased to see me. Eventually the glassmaker's son, Ossinax, appears. He's around nineteen, small for his age, with long hair tied back in a ponytail like most of the lower-class sons of the city. My own hair has never been cut and has trailed down my back since I was young. These days I notice some grey streaks.

"I'm glad you've come," he says, taking me by surprise.

"You are?"

He lowers his voice as if fearful that his father might be listening outside.

"I really don't think Makri stole that money."

"Why not?"

"Because once I asked her to look after a quarter-guran for me and she gave it right back when I asked."

"Why did you need her to look after a quarter-guran?"

"I didn't. It was a bet with some other students. To see how long she'd keep it without stealing it. But then she didn't steal it at all. We were surprised."

"I see."

"I like her," says Ossinax.

He looks a little downcast.

"Though she did punch me after she learned about the bet. But I never told anyone. I didn't want to get her into trouble."

From the tone of Ossinax's voice, I get the impression that he might be harbouring more than some friendly feelings towards Makri. Wouldn't be too strange, really, if only because in a city where women are almost always well wrapped up, Makri never seems to wear enough clothes. She's been sent home from the College because of it on more than one occasion.

"So who else might have taken the money?"

"I don't know. There were a few people around."

Everyone he can remember is on my list, and I've checked them all out.

"Are you sure there was no other student around?"

"Not that I can remember."

"No members of staff?"

"Why would a member of staff steal five gurans?"

"You never know who might need money urgently."

Ossinax doesn't remember seeing any members of staff anywhere near the room in question.

"Professor Toarius was there earlier, but he often walks round the building."

"How much earlier?"

"Around an hour. It was before my philosophy class. He walked along the corridor with Barius."

"Barius?"

"Professor Toarius's son."

"What was he doing there?"

"I don't know. He's a student at the Imperial University. I only saw him once before, when he came down to visit his father. But I'm sure it was him."

No one has mentioned anything about the Professor's son before. That's probably not suspicious. After all, this was more than an hour before the theft. But I'm curious anyway. The Professor didn't say that his son had been there earlier in the day. There again, the Professor didn't mention much before he stormed out of the room. I ask Ossinax if he can tell me anything more about Barius but he can't. He's surprised I'm interested.

"The family is rich. Barius wouldn't have any need to steal five gurans."

"I suppose not."

I let him have my address and tell him to get in touch if he thinks of anything else that might interest me.

"The Avenging Axe? Is that where Makri works?"

"It is."

"Is it a dangerous place?"

"Any place Makri works is a dangerous place."

"Did she really slaughter an Orc lord and all his family when she escaped from the gladiator pits?"

"She did."

"Did she really fight a dragon in the arena?"

I see that Makri has not been above doing a little bragging at the College.

"Yes, she did," I tell him. "And she helped me fight another one, much bigger," I add, not wishing young Ossinax to get the impression that Makri's the only one capable of epic feats in battle. We didn't kill the dragon but we defeated the Orcish forces that accompanied it. Makri dealt the fatal blow by hewing her way through their ranks to kill their commander.

I leave Ossinax looking thoughtful. A servant shows me out under the watchful eye of his father. Outside I can hear the sound of hammering coming from the workshop at the rear. I gaze at the front of the house. "Nice windows. You make them all yourself?" The glassmaker shuts the door. It's hot as Orcish hell. I take a drink from a fountain and look around for someone to sell me a watermelon. I have an urge to visit Barius, son of Professor Toarius. After eating two large watermelons, I still have the urge, so I wave down a landus and tell the driver to take me to Thamlin.

Chapter Ten

It's surprisingly difficult to find Barius. He's not at the Imperial University and no one there has seen him for several days. I traipse uncomfortably around the huge marble halls, asking questions of students and members of staff, but the young man's friends haven't seen him and the tutors and professors aren't keen to give information to an outsider, Tribune or not. When I find myself being lectured at length on the historical duties of the Tribunate by a Professor of Theology, I realise it's time to leave the University. So much learning is making me feel ignorant. The sight of ranks of well-dressed and attentive students sitting in vast lecture halls makes me wonder what they'll make of Makri if she ever manages to force her way into the place. Deputy Consul Cicerius did once hint that he might help her, if circumstances allowed, but he needed a favour from her at the time. I doubt he'd come through with any real assistance if it came down to it.

Barius still lives in the family home, so that should be my next destination, though I'm not looking forward to another encounter with Professor Toarius. The Professor will be down on me like a bad spell if I start bothering his household. Toarius belongs to an important family and has a lot of influential friends. Being a professor doesn't by itself give a man high status, but Toarius's family own a lot of land outside the city and have been wealthy for longer than anyone can remember. Too bad, I muse, as I head towards his villa. During my career as an Investigator, I've already offended most important people in the city, so another one probably doesn't matter that much.

Which reminds me. I've been meaning to make some enquiries about Lisutaris's secretary. I'm curious as to why the Sorcerer is so protective towards her. I break off my mission to call in on a tavern owner I know who used to be employed as head of stables by Tas of the Eastern Lightning. When that Sorcerer handed in his toga a year or so back, the stableman found himself out of a job and ended up putting his savings into a tavern, which suits him well enough. I once got his son off a charge of assault after a street fracas and he's helped me once or twice before with his knowledge of the staff and servants of our city's Sorcerers.

"Lisutaris's secretary? Sure I remember her. Avenaris. Nervous little thing. Daughter of Lisutaris's older brother. When he was killed in the war, Lisutaris took her in. Looked after her ever since. What's she been up to?"

"Nothing that I know of. What does she have to be nervous about?"

"Who knows?"

He can't tell me any more. Avenaris has never been in trouble and is a loyal employee. No scandal, no boyfriends. Just nervous. I thank him, leave him enough money for a few drinks, and get back to my quest.

Professor Toarius lives in Thamlin. I'm amazed as always at how neat and clean everything is. No rubbish on the streets, no beggars on the corners, no stray dogs looking hungrily for food. The pavements are covered in the pale yellow and green tiles that are a distinctive feature of Turai's wealthy areas, and every large house is set well back from the road, fronted by extensive gardens. The streets are quiet, with well-behaved servants carrying provisions home to their employers, and a visible presence of Civil Guards, here to keep out undesirables.

When an official-looking carriage pulls up alongside me, my first thought is that I've been deemed undesirable. I'm astonished when the curtains of the carriage open and the Consul himself beckons to me. I've met Consul Kalius before but I wouldn't expect Turai's highest official to be searching the streets for me.

"Get in," instructs Kalius.

I get in.

"Where are we going?"

"We're not going anywhere."

Kalius must be sixty years old. His toga is lined with gold as befits his rank, and he wears it with pride. As Turanian Consuls go, he's moderately well regarded. If he's not exactly as sharp as an Elf's ear, then neither is he the most foolish we've had, and while he lacks Cicerius's reputation for fierce incorruptibility, at least he hasn't been flagrant in taking bribes, and he's a lot more charismatic than his deputy.

"I wish to talk with you. Here will do as well as any-where."

I'm puzzled by the meeting. I ask the Consul if he just happened to be riding by.

"I was searching for you. My Sorcerer located you and I rode quickly to intercept you."

If the Consul has actually used a Sorcerer to locate me, I have to be in trouble over something. The authorities generally don't use their Sorcerers for trivial matters.

"What task are you performing for Lisutaris, Mistress of the Sky?"

I'm not sure what to say. I can't possibly reveal Lisutaris's reason for hiring me. It strikes me fully for the first time that Lisutaris is withholding some tremendously important information from the state, information that really should not have been withheld, and I'm now fully implicated. If disaster strikes Turai because the errant Sorcerer has lost the pendant and I'm held to have been responsible for its non-recovery, I'll be lucky to avoid spending the rest of my life on a slave galley.

I consider denying that Lisutaris has hired me but reject it as too risky, given the Consul's many sources of information. It's time to lie, something I pride myself on my talent for.

"She hired me to find some personal papers."

"What sort of papers?"

"Her diary."

Kalius regards me coolly for some moments.

"Her diary?"

"Yes. She lost it at the chariot races. Naturally it's a sensitive matter. No important Sorcerer wants details of her daily thoughts placed before the public. You know how cruel people can be. And the *Renowned and Truthful Chronicle* would probably publish the whole thing if it fell into their hands."

Kalius isn't looking convinced.

"Lisutaris hired you to find her diary? I find that hard to believe."

"Diaries are sensitive objects, Consul. I believe hers may contain several love poems. Naturally she's anxious that no one should see them."

"Are you telling me that Turai's most important Sorcerer has been wasting her time writing love poems?"

I raise my palms towards the sky.

"Are love poems a waste of time? Who can say? In the tavern where I live there are various persons deeply enmeshed in affairs of the—"

"I am not interested in the squalid affairs that may go on in the Avenging Axe," says Kalius, acidly.

It's gratifying to realise that the Consul actually remembers where I live. He did come there one time, to harangue me, but I thought he'd probably have forgotten. I struggle on with my story.

"Lisutaris needed a man of discretion to work on her behalf. I'm sure you understand. Really I shouldn't be telling you this and must ask you to make sure the information goes no further."

"I have been informed by our Civil Guard that you have been involved in a great many deaths in recent days. Are you aware that earlier today six men were found hacked to death near to the pleasure gardens?"

"I wasn't. Does it concern me?"

"It concerns Lisutaris. I have information that an Investigator named Demanius was quickly on the scene and I have further information that Demanius is involved in some matter concerning Lisutaris."

"Demanius? The name is vaguely familiar. Who hired him?"

Kalius won't tell me who has hired Demanius, and nor will he tell me how he knows that Demanius is working on anything that concerns Lisutaris, but I take his information as reliable. The Consul's office has its own efficient intelligence services. It is distressing to learn that another six men have died. More distressing that Demanius was on the scene and I knew nothing about it.

"It seems unlikely that so many murders would have occurred during the pursuit of a diary, no matter how many poems it may contain," says the Consul.

"I haven't been involved in these deaths, Consul. They just happened while I was there. Following up leads on the diary naturally led me into several insalubrious venues. Not the sort of place I'd normally wish to visit, but an Investigator has little choice. I believe there may have been some violence but it was nothing to do with me. Or Lisutaris."

Kalius wears a small gold ring on his right hand, an official seal, one of the emblems of his office as chief representative of the King. He fingers it and looks thoughtful.

"If I learn that you are lying to me, Investigator, you will be punished."

I assure him I'm not lying. I'm eager to be on my way but Kalius hasn't finished with me.

"When Cicerius made you a Tribune, I understand he made it clear that the appointment was honorary."

"He did."

"And yet you are using the historical powers of the Tribunate against the express will of the government."

There's no point lying on this one.

"I felt it was justified," I say.

"Last time you foolishly used these powers was there not an attempt to assassinate you?"

"There was."

"I would have thought that would have been sufficient discouragement," says Kalius. "Politics in this city is not to be entered by the likes of you. Be warned. Your powers are purely notional. If you find yourself in trouble because of your actions, the government will not support you."

Kalius dismisses me from his carriage. His driver takes up the reins and canters off. I wonder what sort of punishment Kalius has in mind. I wonder if I should just pack a bag and leave the city. I wonder why they don't build taverns in Thamlin. I really need a beer.

I can't find a landus for hire anywhere so I have to walk a long way back towards the centre of the city. Here the streets are unpaved and I'm soon choking on the dust and cursing the heat. Halfway along Moon and Stars Boulevard another carriage pulls up. It's a big day for finding Thraxas in your carriage. Lisutaris opens the door and beckons me in. Her conveyance is luxuriously furnished but smells strongly of thazis.

"Find me with a spell?"

She nods.

"I think I have located the pendant."

"Just as well. The Consul suspects you've lost it."

I describe my recent encounter. Lisutaris is greatly disturbed, not least by my informing the Consul that she's been writing love poetry. Her elegant features take on a rather piqued air.

"Couldn't you think of anything more convincing?"

"I didn't have time to think. Anyway, it's not that unbelievable. Sorcerers are occasionally poetic. And you've never married. Who knows if you might be pining for someone?"

"I'm starting to believe that Harmon Half Elf was right about you."

"Harmon? What's he been saying?"

"That you're an imbecile."

Lisutaris looks like she has a great deal more to say on the subject, but at this moment the call for afternoon prayers rings out over the city. It's a legal requirement for all Turanian

citizens to pray three times a day, and while the last thing I
want to do right now is get down on my knees, I don't have
a choice. It's illegal even to remain in a carriage, so, muffling
our frustration, Lisutaris and I both clamber out into the
street to join those others also unfortunate enough not to be
indoors. Lisutaris frowns at the prospect of kneeling in the
dust and getting her gown dirty.

"But perhaps I could do with some divine help," she mutters,
shooting me a glance which may imply that she no longer has
total confidence in me as an Investigator. We pray in silence.
Or rather pretend to pray. I'm too busy seething with resentment over Harmon Half Elf calling me an imbecile. He might
be a very powerful Sorcerer, but I've never considered him
that intelligent. The call goes up for prayers to end.

"I'm going to have something to say to Harmon Half Elf,"
I say, hauling myself to my feet.

"You would be unwise to offend Harmon," replies Lisutaris.

"Unwise? You think I'd worry about offending that pointy-
eared charlatan? He wouldn't be the first Sorcerer I've punched
in the face before they had time to utter a spell."

Lisutaris starts hunting in her bag for some thazis.

"If I'd realised you were so unstable I'd never have hired
you."

"I'm not unstable. I just don't like Sorcerers calling me a
moron."

"The word was imbecile."

"Or imbecile."

We set off at a fast pace through the city. Lisutaris tells me
that though she is still unable to locate the pendant directly,
she has tracked Sarin to a warehouse at the docks.

"And I've also traced a powerful user of magic heading there.
I believe it must be connected to the pendant."

"Probably. Any idea who the powerful user of magic is?"

Lisutaris shakes her head.

"An aura I am not familiar with."

We're making good progress down the boulevard, and cross the river at a brisk pace. Lisutaris's driver is an experienced hand and wends his way through the crush of delivery wagons with a skill I can admire.

"Does Kalius really think I've lost the pendant?"

"I'm not certain. He suspects you're in some deep trouble. He may know nothing more. But that would be enough to worry the government, with you being head of the Sorcerers Guild."

"He's bound to ask to see the pendant at my ball," moans the Sorcerer.

"Perhaps if I was there I could divert him in some manner?"

"I doubt it," says Lisutaris, and lights another thazis stick.

I sit in silence for the rest of the journey. Lisutaris idly wipes the dust from her gown. Like her rainbow cloak, it's of the highest quality. The Mistress of the Sky is an extremely wealthy woman. She inherited a vast fortune from her father, a prosperous landowner who greatly increased his fortune after he entered the Senate, as Senators tend to do. It's unusual for Turai's Sorcerers to come from the very highest stratum of society—sorcery, like trade, is generally thought to be beneath their dignity—but Lisutaris, as the youngest child in the family, was left free to choose her own path while her two older brothers were groomed for their roles in society. Her father may not have been overly pleased when she began to show an aptitude for sorcery, but with two male siblings already growing up respectably he didn't forbid her to carry on with her studies.

In normal circumstances, Lisutaris would have ended up as a

working Sorcerer with a modest income, but both her brothers were unfortunately killed in the last Orc war, leaving her as sole heir to the huge family fortune. Since then she's carried on her dual role as member of the aristocracy and powerful Sorcerer without causing too much scandal in a city which frowns on the unusual. Her fine record during the war still protects her from criticism, even though her enormous appetite for thazis must be widely known to her peers. *The Renowned and Truthful Chronicle of All the World's Events* has occasionally made some snide references to her remaining unmarried, but even that is not regarded as too outlandish for a Sorcerer. Sorcerers are allowed a degree of eccentricity, particularly a Sorcerer who hurled back regiments of Orc warriors with her powerful spells. Furthermore, her recent election to head of the Sorcerers Guild, an organisation covering most of the Sorcerers in the west, has brought great honour to Turai, and a degree of security.

Our carriage pulls up alongside a tall warehouse not far from the harbour.

"Sarin is inside," says Lisutaris.

I don't ask her how she knows. Lisutaris has powers of seeing I could never aspire to even if I'd studied all my life.

"Fine," I say. "How do we get past the centaurs?"

"Centaurs?"

Three centaurs are currently walking round the corner, these being half man, half horse, and absolutely never seen in Turai. They're even rarer than unicorns. I met some in the fairy glade, but apart from that I'm not sure they exist anywhere in the world. We stare at them, more or less open-mouthed in surprise.

"They just cannot be here," says Lisutaris. "A centaur would never visit this city."

"And if they did they wouldn't come to Twelve Seas."

"The human environment is anathema to them."

As we watch the centaurs pause in front of the warehouse, I wonder if I should draw my sword. Centaurs can be tough creatures when they're roused. I know, I've seen them fight. However, they pay us no attention but carry on round the warehouse, disappearing around the far corner, human heads held high, horse tails flapping behind them.

We walk cautiously to the corner of the warehouse and peer round. No centaurs are in sight.

"They can't have disappeared," mutters Lisutaris. "I should alert the authorities."

"No footprints."

"What?"

"No footprints. Real centaurs would have left plenty of marks in the dust. It was some sort of apparition. Is there sorcery being used here?"

"Yes," replies Lisutaris. "But I'm not sure what type, or by who."

Three mysterious centaurs are interesting enough, but we have business to attend to. I suggest we check out the warehouse before Sarin also disappears. Inside it's dark. Lisutaris draws a short staff from her cloak and mutters a word of power, and light floods to the furthest corner of the building. All around are crates and boxes.

"Upstairs," says Lisutaris.

I follow her up the wooden stairs, all the time keeping a sharp look-out for Sarin the Merciless.

"She's deadly with a crossbow," I whisper.

"I'll protect you," says Lisutaris.

I'd meant it more as a warning than a plea for protection but I don't argue. I'm concerned about the powerful user of magic that Lisutaris detected heading our way. You never know who might just be carrying the one spell that will pierce your protection.

We climb up a long way. Inside the warehouse it's hot as Orcish hell, and by the third flight of stairs sweat is pouring down the inside of my tunic. My intuition, already buzzing after the centaurs, starts going into overdrive. Danger is close. Lisutaris dims her illuminated staff and steps carefully through the doorway that leads off on to the top floor. Suddenly there's a humming sound in the air. I duck instinctively but Lisutaris remains upright, hand in the air. A crossbow bolt bounces off her magical energy field and clatters harmlessly on the floor.

Lisutaris boosts her illuminated staff to full power again, and there in the far corner I see Sarin urgently loading another bolt into her weapon. I raise my sword and charge at her with the intention of removing her head from her shoulders before she can fire again. Which I'm confident of doing. I might not be able to magically deflect a crossbow bolt, but when it comes to street fighting Thraxas is number one chariot. I aim a blow at Sarin's neck and I swear my sword is no more than two inches away from decapitating her when I'm suddenly picked up bodily as if by an invisible hand and flung across the warehouse, where I land in a breathless heap, bruised and confused. As I haul myself to my feet, two things catch my eye. One, Sarin has now reloaded her crossbow. Two, Glixius Dragon Killer has ascended the stairs behind us. Glixius is a really powerful Sorcerer, the most powerful criminal Sorcerer I've ever encountered, at least of the Human variety. He motions with his hand and Lisutaris goes flying through the air.

Trusting that Lisutaris can look after herself, I throw myself sword first at Sarin just as she's pulling the trigger of her crossbow. My blade connects with the tip of her weapon, sending the bolt upwards into the ceiling but in the process wrenching my blade from my hands. Sarin immediately drops the crossbow and kicks me in the face and I get a painful reminder that the last time I encountered her she proved to be a formidable opponent in hand-to-hand combat. I can feel blood spurting from my nose. I ignore it and step forward with my fists raised. I've nothing fancy in mind, just use my bulk to overwhelm her. Sarin kicks me again and leaps backwards but I keep on going till she's up against the wall, and then I connect with a punch which drops her like a drunken Elf falling from a tree.

I pick up my sword, and gaze down at her prostrate form with some satisfaction. I owed her that. I'm just wondering if it would be appropriate to give her a few hefty kicks when the invisible hand again picks me up, and hurls me backwards through a window, leaving me, some boxes and a great deal of broken glass plummeting to earth from a height of more than a hundred feet.

Chapter Eleven

Fifty feet from the ground, I'm not feeling confident. There's a paved road outside the warehouse and I'm plummeting towards it at an ungodly rate. I curse Glixius, Sarin, Lisutaris and the hostile fates who've had it in for me since the day I was born. This takes me down to about ten feet. I close my eyes. I come to a gentle halt. Benevolent sorcery, presumably from Lisutaris, has rescued me. I land lightly on my feet, sword still in hand, and immediately charge back into the warehouse, ready to show Glixius Dragon Killer that I'm not a man you can toss out of a high window without suffering the consequences.

Inside the situation is confused. More people have entered the building. There's a full-scale battle going on all up the wooden staircase. I recognise several local Brotherhood men struggling with opponents whom I guess to be from the Society of Friends. Approaching fast are five or six uniformed men from Palace Security, the King's own intelligence service.

"Quite a commotion, Thraxas?" says a voice from behind me.

It's Demanius, from the Venarius Investigation Agency.

"What are you doing here?" I demand.

"Same as you," replies Demanius.

"I'm not doing anything."

"Then neither am I."

Above our heads the fight intensifies. Some of the struggling figures are forced off the staircase on to the floors that lead off to either side, and I make an effort to fight my way through. My client is upstairs, currently in combat with Glixius Dragon Killer and Sarin the Merciless. I should be at her side.

When four men from the Society of Friends appear before me, swords raised, I get the fleeting feeling that I wish Makri was here to lend her strength to mine. Though if she was, she'd probably end up killing the men from Palace Security as well as my opponents and things would only get worse. Makri has no self-control once she gets her axe out.

As it turns out, I'm not alone. Demanius arrives at my side and we confront our foes together. The Society of Friends men are far from their home territory. It's dangerous for them to venture south of the river where the Brotherhood hold sway, and I'd guess these thugs, seeing their mission go wrong, are keen to depart as swiftly as possible. I'm about to offer them the opportunity to do just that, thereby avoiding a messy conflict, when from behind me comes the sound of a Civil Guard's whistle. I risk a swift glance backwards. Twenty or so Guards, led by Captain Rallee, are now streaming into the warehouse.

Intent on not being captured by the Guards, the Society of Friends men lose interest in me. They turn and flee up the stairs. I follow them with Demanius at my heels.

With the warehouse now full of the Brotherhood, the Society of Friends, Palace Security, Civil Guards, plus assorted Investigators, Sorcerers and murderous adventurers, I'd say that I've finally blown it as far as keeping Lisutaris's problem a secret goes. When I reach the second floor and find Harmon Half Elf floating in through an open window, rainbow cloak billowing in the breeze, it strikes me that Lisutaris, Mistress of the Sky, might be in for some tough questioning from the Sorcerers Guild if she ever finishes her session with Palace Security. All this being dependent on Lisutaris remaining alive, of course. I ignore the struggling masses and keep heading up the stairs.

I'm just beneath the top floor when there's a flash and a shattering explosion rips through the building. Wood and stone rain down on my head. The floorboards cry in protest as mystical forces start to rip the place apart. All around voices are raised in panic as the warehouse starts to sway.

"Get out of here!" yells Demanius.

I keep on going. I have to rescue my client. Her sorcerous conflict with Glixius Dragon Killer has brought about the destruction of the warehouse, and for all I know she might be lying unconscious with Sarin the Merciless standing over her, crossbow in hand.

The walls are now starting to buckle. Strips of wood fall around my shoulders as I rush into the room at the very top of the warehouse. Fire has broken out and smoke is now pouring from the walls, quickly taking hold. As I reach the final room the roof starts caving in and I'm knocked off my feet by a great beam which pins me to the floor. I struggle to free myself, vainly.

"Thraxas?"

Lisutaris is standing over me, looking calm and untroubled.

"I gave you a safe landing. Why did you come back?"

"To rescue you."

I think Lisutaris smiles. In the ever-thickening smoke, it's hard to tell.

"Thank you," she says.

The Sorceress waves her hand. The beam flies off me. I haul myself to my feet, with some difficulty.

"We have to get out," I gasp. "Building's coming apart."

There's a blast that sounds like a squadron of war dragons crashing to earth and the warehouse caves in. For the second time in the space of a few minutes I find myself one hundred feet off the ground with nothing in the way to break my fall.

Lisutaris is beside me in mid-air. We're both hovering gently. It's quite a pleasant sensation.

"Did you really come back to rescue me?"

"Yes."

"But the building was collapsing. It was foolish."

"I have a duty towards my clients."

The breeze blows smoke from the wreckage around our faces. From this elevation I have a really good view of Twelve Seas. It doesn't look any better.

We start to sink, very gently.

"Are those Civil Guards?" asks Lisutaris.

"I'm afraid so. Palace Security is here as well. And Harmon Half Elf."

"What does he want?"

"Maybe the Sorcerers Guild is getting curious."

Lisutaris frowns. Her long hair flutters in the wind.

"Are you saying my secret is out?"

"They have their suspicions. What happened to Glixius and Sarin?"

Lisutaris doesn't know. She didn't find it difficult to defeat Glixius in a contest of sorcerous strength but she was unable to prevent him from bringing down the building with a blasting spell which allowed him to escape.

"As for Sarin, I don't know."

With any luck she'll have perished horribly. By this time we're almost at ground level. A lot of people are waiting for us to land.

"What am I going to say?" asks Lisutaris.

"Say nothing."

"Nothing? That's hardly going to convince anyone."

"You outrank all these people. Till the Consul himself has you under oath in a courtroom, deny everything. Let me do the talking."

The corners of Lisutaris's mouth turn downwards.

"I fear I'm doomed. But thank you again for your rescue attempt."

We land a short distance away from the burning warehouse and are immediately surrounded. Everyone is asking questions at once. Captain Rallee is particularly insistent. This is his patch and he doesn't like having it disturbed by armed gangs burning down warehouses.

"Or did you destroy the warehouse with sorcery?" he says, directing his gaze towards Lisutaris.

Harmon Half Elf stands to one side, waiting his turn. As far as I know, Turai's senior Sorcerers have no power to officially censure the leader of their guild, but it's going to destroy Lisutaris's reputation if they turn against her. A man who seems to be in charge of the operatives from Palace Security—which is headed, unfortunately, by Rittius, a great enemy of mine—adds his voice to the others. Everyone looks to Lisutaris, waiting for an explanation. Desperate measures being called for, I step to the fore and hold up my hand.

"Official Tribune's business," I state, loudly. "Lisutaris is here at my request, helping me with an inquiry. As such, I forbid her to talk of today's events. A full report will be presented to the Consul in good time."

There's something of a stunned silence. Civil Guards and Palace Security don't expect to be given orders by Private Investigators. However, for some reason which it would take a historian to explain, the Tribune's powers were very great, and could only be overruled by a full meeting of the Senate. It's little wonder that the authorities eventually let the institution fall into disuse. Their powers were never legally rescinded, however, which means that as long as I'm a Tribune they're stuck with it. Captain Rallee knows enough about the law not to argue, but as I lead Lisutaris away from the scene he draws me to one side.

"You're digging yourself a pretty big hole, Thraxas. I don't exactly know what's going on, but if you're covering up for Lisutaris, the government is going to come down on you like a bad spell. And don't expect her to stick up for you when you're being indicted before a Senate committee."

"I won't."

"You know anything about any centaurs? We got a report from some crazy person that three of them were wandering around."

"They were. I saw them, briefly."

The captain doesn't like this at all.

"Yesterday it was unicorns, now it's centaurs. At first I thought it was the dwa talking, but now I'm not so sure."

He turns to Lisutaris.

"You know of any reason why strange magical creatures might be suddenly appearing all over the city?"

"I have no idea," responds Lisutaris, which ends the matter. A Guards captain can't get tough with the head of the

Sorcerers Guild. Lisutaris turns to go and I follow her. Captain Rallee calls after us.

"I made a quick body count in the warehouse. Six men dead. How many more before it ends?"

"I have no idea," I call back, uncomfortably.

"I've got a bet down on twenty; how's that looking?"

Declining to reply, I usher Lisutaris up the paved road on to which I almost plunged from a great height. Behind us the fire wagons have arrived and are doing good work putting out the blaze. They train their horses not to fear fire. It's a marvellous institution. The Civil Guards are arresting every remaining gang member, and Harmon Half Elf stares after us. Let him stare. I haven't forgiven him for calling me an imbecile. We leave the scene in Lisutaris's carriage.

"I believe that there is no extradition treaty between Turai and Abelesi," says Lisutaris.

"So?"

"I'm just wondering where the best place to flee might be."

"Flee? Put the thought out of your mind. We're not beaten yet."

"We have less than two days to retrieve an item which has so far eluded all our efforts. And even if we do find it, I'm still ruined. There's no way of keeping it secret now."

Lisutaris draws a thazis stick from a large pocket inside her gown.

"Don't despair. I don't give up easily. Besides, none of these people really know what's going on. Till you admit you've lost the pendant, everything is rumour and supposition, and the head of the Sorcerers Guild doesn't have to answer to rumour. Just keep denying everything."

"And what if someone else retrieves the pendant?"

"Then I'll be joining you in Abelesi. But it's not going to happen. I'll find it."

Lisutaris isn't convinced. Neither am I, but I'm stubborn.

"Any theories regarding the centaurs?"

"No. I can't explain their appearance, What did Captain Rallee mean when he asked you about how many bodies?"

"I expect he was just seeking information for his report. You know these Guards, always like to get their figures correct."

Lisutaris turns her gaze fully upon me.

"I am head of the Sorcerers Guild," she says.

Meaning, I think, that you can't fob her off with a lie.

"Word got out that I was on a big case," I admit. "It was the fault of this weird woman called Dandelion who talks to dolphins. She read in the stars that I was about to be involved in a bloodbath, and ever since then the regulars at the Avenging Axe have been taking bets on how many bodies there will be before it ends."

Lisutaris's eyes widen. I get ready to leap from the carriage. Unexpectedly, she starts to laugh.

"They're placing bets?"

She seems to find this funny.

"Here we are, trying to keep the news from the Consul, and down in the Avenging Axe they're placing bets."

"I have strongly advised them to desist."

"Why? How much has Makri gone in for?"

"Fourteen bodies."

"Too few, I fear," says Lisutaris.

"It is. I think we're up to twenty-one now."

"What odds are being offered?"

"Fifty to one for the exact total, twenty to one if you get within three."

"You still have the money I gave you to retrieve the pendant? Then put me down for thirty-five," she says.

"Are you sure?"

"Of course. After my recent losses at the chariot races, why should I pass up this opportunity?"

"Because the whole thing is unethical."

"A bet is a bet," says Lisutaris.

I feel a great weight lifting off me. I realise why I've been so angry about the whole thing. It's because I've felt unable to place a bet. Here am I, Thraxas, number one chariot among Twelve Seas gamblers, caught up in a fine sporting contest yet unable, for reasons of ethics, to participate. No wonder I felt bad. Now, with the sanction of my client, I'm free to join in. It's a great relief.

"Fine. But do you really think we'll reach thirty-five?"

"At least," says Lisutaris. "I can feel it."

As the carriage trundles along, I get down to some serious calculations as to where I'm going to place my own bet. I'll show these scum at the Avenging Axe what a real gambler is capable of. Young Moxalan will regret ever entering the bookmaking business by the time I've cleaned him out.

Lisutaris drops me off at Quintessence Street. The woman who sells fish and the man who's set up a stall for sharpening blades are arguing again. I've more to worry about than bad-tempered vendors. Like Makri, for instance, who once more is sheltering in my office.

"Are you going to spend every break in here till that freak Dandelion leaves?"

"I might."

"You see, that's one of your problems, Makri. You tolerate these weird sort of people and where does it get you? They take advantage. In a city like Turai it doesn't pay to tolerate people. You have to be tough."

"I am tough."

"With a sword, yes. With down-and-outs, not nearly tough enough."

"Doesn't your religion say you should be kind to the poor?" counters Makri.

"Probably. I never learned much about it."

"What about your three prayers a day? What are you praying for?"

"Self-advancement, same as everyone else."

"I'm glad I don't have a religion," says Makri.

"That's because you're a Barbarian who grew up without the benefit of a proper education."

"I'm educated enough not to continue with this conversation, you fat hypocrite," says Makri.

She produces two thazis sticks which she's stolen from behind the bar. We light one each and smoke them in silence. Relaxed from the effects of the thazis, I describe today's events.

"All in all, another disaster."

"How many dead does that make?" asks Makri.

"Twenty-one. But there's every indication that there's more to come. So I figure we should place a few bets somewhere around the thirty mark, and maybe take a punt at forty, just in case things really get rough."

"Pardon?" says Makri.

"Of course, you'll have to put the bet on for me. Moxalan isn't going to accept a wager from me, he'd disqualify me for having too much inside information."

Makri is looking baffled.

"I'm getting the feeling I've missed something again. You've spent the last two days berating me for gambling on your investigation, and now you're telling me I have to place a bet on your behalf? What changed?"

"Nothing."

"What about the ethical problems?"

"I leave ethics to the philosophers. Lisutaris wants to put money on, you'd better do that as well."

"Okay. As long as I can hide in your rooms from Dandelion."

"If you must. I may need to borrow a little money."

"What about all the money Lisutaris gave you?"

"I used it to pay the rent and buy a case of klee."

"I don't have any money to spare," claims Makri.

"Yes you do. You've been putting away your tips to pay for your examinations and I happen to know you've more than a hundred gurans secreted in your room for that purpose."

"How dare you—"

I hold up my hand.

"Before you launch into a diatribe, I might remind you that it wasn't too long ago I found you trying to steal the emergency fifty-guran coin I was keeping under my couch. Furthermore, I've helped you out with money on numerous occasions, not to mention steering you in the right direction when it came to placing several astute wagers, so get off your moral high horse and make with the money. With my inside information and your cash we're on to a certainty, and you'll win enough money to pay for your examinations this year and next year and probably buy a new axe as well."

"Well, all right," says Makri, "but don't ever lecture me about anything again."

"I wouldn't dream of it."

"Are you any closer to actually recovering the pendant?"

"No. It's frustrating. I thought it was going to be easy. Sorcerers. You can't trust them."

The heat makes me drowsy. When Makri goes back to work I don't fight the urge to go to sleep. I waken hungry and head downstairs to fill up with Tanrose's stew. I hope she's patched things up with Gurd. I depend so completely on her cooking that I dread her leaving the tavern. Moxalan is in the bar and Makri gives me a discreet nod, indicating that she's placed our bet.

Despite the usual hubbub from the early-evening customers, something seems to be missing. No friendly aroma of stew. No smell of food at all. A strange sensation washes over me and I find myself trembling, something that's never happened even in the face of the most deadly opponent. I fear the worst.

"Where's Tanrose? Where's the food?"

"She left," says Gurd, and draws a pint with such viciousness that the beer pump nearly disintegrates in his hand.

"What about the food?"

"Tanrose left," repeats Gurd, slamming the tankard down in front of an alarmed customer.

"Did she leave any food?"

"No. She just left."

"Why?"

"Makri told her to."

"What?"

"I did not tell her to leave," says Makri.

My trembling is getting worse.

"Someone tell me what happened!" I yell. "Where has Tanrose gone?"

"Back to her mother," says Gurd, flatly. "Makri told her to."

"This is a really inaccurate description of events," protests Makri. "I merely suggested that she take a little time to sort out her feelings for Gurd and then speak to him frankly."

Gurd sags like a man with a fatal wound. I get the urge to bury my face in my hands.

"What happened then?"

"She told me she was fed up with working for a man who was too mean-spirited to appreciate the things she did for him," groans Gurd. "Then she packed her bags and left."

Makri studies the floor around her feet.

"It wasn't the result I was expecting," she says.

"Why couldn't you leave well alone?" I yell at her. "Now look what you've done! Tanrose has gone!"

Makri looks exasperated.

"I was only trying to help. Like you suggested."

"Thraxas suggested it?" says Gurd.

"I did no such thing. Makri, you vile Orcish wench, do you realise what you've done?"

Makri's mouth opens wide in shock.

"Did you just call me a vile Orcish wench?"

"I did. And of all the ridiculous things you've done since you arrived here to plague us, this is the worst. Now Gurd will be as miserable as a Niojan whore for the rest of his life and I'll starve to death."

"Why couldn't you leave things alone?" cries Gurd.

After my Orcish slur Makri's first impulse was to reach for her sword, but faced with fresh criticism from Gurd she's confused.

"I was just trying to—"

Dandelion suddenly arrives and throws herself into the conversation.

"Thraxas, I have terrible news."

"I've already heard," I say. "We have to bring her back."

"Who?"

"Tanrose, of course."

"Has she left?" says Dandelion.

"Of course. It's terrible news."

"Why?"

"What do you mean, why? This woman cooks the best stew in Turai."

Dandelion sniffs.

"I do not partake of the flesh of animals," she says.

I raise my fist.

"Don't you dare punch Dandelion," says Makri, getting in between us.

"Maybe I should punch you."

"Just try it."

Makri raises her hands and sinks into her defensive posture.

"I can't live without Tanrose," says Gurd. I've never heard him sounding so distressed. I once pulled three arrows out of his ribs and he never so much as complained.

"You're not listening to my news," says Dandelion.

"If it's something to do with the stars, I'm not interested."

"But the stars are sacred!"

"I'm not interested."

There's no putting the woman off. Dandelion is practically jumping up and down in her frenzied eagerness to tell me something.

"The most serious of warnings! Last night there were flashes in the sky the like of which I've never seen!"

"So?"

"It was as if the skies above the beach were on fire!"

"Will you stop giving me warnings? They've already caused enough trouble."

Dandelion looks hurt. She fingers her necklace—a ridiculous affair made of seashells—and mumbles something about only trying to help. Voices are raised everywhere as people now seek to give their opinions on the various topics on offer. Gurd, Makri and myself all find ourselves bombarded with suggestions. Most people seem to think that Gurd should go and propose marriage to Tanrose immediately, but there's a vocal faction who want to know if it's true that Lisutaris has promised to kill anyone who gets in the way of her illicit love affair.

"Lisutaris is not having an illicit love affair."

"Then why has she hired you to retrieve her diary? Word is it's full of incriminating poetry."

"How many people are likely to get in her way?" asks Parax. "Are we talking three figures?"

"If she's been spurned," muses a docker, "she might get very violent. You know what women are like when they're spurned."

Gurd abandons all hope and sits down heavily behind the bar, unwilling or unable to even draw a jar of ale. Makri, remembering that I called her a vile Orcish wench, is now threatening to kill me. I inform her I'll be happy to send her head back to her mother, if she has a mother, which I doubt. It would seem that things could hardly get worse when a young government official in a crisp white toga strides into the bar. Ignoring my drawn sword, he hands me a document.

"What's this?"

"Citation of cowardice."

"What?"

"You've been called before a committee of the Senate to account for your behaviour at the Battle of Sanasa."

My head swims. The Battle of Sanasa was all of seventeen years ago.

"What are you talking about?"

"It is alleged that you discarded your shield and fled the field."

There's a gasp from the assembled drinkers in the tavern. Discarding one's shield on the field of battle is one of the most serious charges that can be faced by a Turanian citizen. Never did I imagine that I could be accused of such a thing. The world has truly gone insane.

Chapter Twelve

I erupt in a volcanic fury.

"Discarded my shield? Me? I practically won the Battle of Sanasa single-handed, you young dog. If it wasn't for me you wouldn't be walking round this city in a toga. You wouldn't have a city to walk around. Who makes this allegation?"

"Vadinex, also a participant in the battle," answers the official.

"We'll see about that," I roar, and head for the door, sword still in hand. I wave it for extra effect. No one accuses me of cowardice. Gurd brings me to a halt by placing his arms around me and wedging his foot against a table.

"Where are you going?" he demands.

"To kill Vadinex, of course. No one accuses me of discarding my shield."

"Killing Vadinex won't help."

"Of course it will help. Now get your arms off me. I have some killing to do."

"They'll hang you."

I try to break free from Gurd's mighty grip. Makri is looking on, amused.

"Not that I mind you being hanged for murder, Thraxas, what with you calling me a vile Orcish wench and being intolerably rude, but isn't this similar to when you told me not to kill Professor Toarius?"

"It's not the same at all. Vadinex has impugned my honour."

"Toarius impugned mine."

"I don't care!" I roar, and renew my struggle with Gurd.

"You'll be arrested and then you won't be able to help Lisutaris."

I cease struggling. In truth, I'm finding it hard to break free of Gurd's grasp. He always was an unusually strong man, and he's kept himself in better shape than me. He starts hauling me back towards the bar.

"Would they really hang Thraxas if he killed Vadinex?" asks Makri.

"Yes," replies Gurd.

"Then it sounds like a good plan. Let him go."

Gurd shoots a very fierce and barbaric scowl in Makri's direction.

"We don't need any more advice from you. Go and serve customers."

Throughout all this the government official has remained calmly waiting for an opportunity to speak, and when he does so the tavern falls silent. There's still something about a man in a toga that induces respect.

"I must tell you that a man facing such a charge can no longer participate in any official duty. So you are forbidden by law to use the office of Tribune. Furthermore, your Investigator's licence, being granted by the Consul's office on behalf of the King, is temporarily revoked until such time as you be either cleared, in which case it shall be renewed, or convicted, in which case it will be revoked."

"Are you saying I can't investigate?"

"That is correct."

"How long for?"

He doesn't know. Until my case is heard by the Senate committee. This could take months. Possibly years. Unless you're a man with influence in this city, legal cases can take a very long time to come to court.

The official departs, leaving me to contemplate the terrible baseness of the accusations. Gurd directs Makri to look after the bar and leads me into the back room, where he pours me a hefty glass of klee. I drink it in one and he refills the glass.

"Thanks, Gurd. For stopping me going to kill Vadinex. It would have been foolish. Though I still want to do it."

"Of course," says Gurd. "That's what I'd want to do if anyone accused me of cowardice. Back in the north I'd have killed him already. But things are different here."

I look at Gurd with some surprise.

"When did you become the responsible citizen?"

"When I bought this tavern and started paying taxes."

I've known Gurd for so long. I always think of him with his axe in his hand, hewing at the enemy. Somehow it hadn't quite struck me how much he's changed. Matured, I suppose. Not that he's a man who'd avoid a fight if it came along, as he's demonstrated various times on my behalf in the past few years. Gurd senses my thoughts.

"Don't worry. If you can't clear your name by the law, I'll help you kill Vadinex and we can flee the city together."

I take another glass of klee. The way things are going we might find ourselves heading south with Lisutaris. She'd be a good companion for an outlaw. No problem lighting campfires in the wilderness. Gurd asks me if I know what's behind this unfortunate turn of events.

"I used my Tribune's powers to protect Lisutaris. It meant putting a block on the Civil Guards and Palace Security. I should have known I couldn't meddle with powerful people like that. Someone's out for revenge. Probably Rittius, head of Palace Security. He's had it in for me for years. It was bound to happen."

Gurd attempts to reassure me. "No one who knows you would ever believe you threw away your shield and fled the battlefield."

"What about people that don't know me? This will be all over the city. Some people will believe it."

In a place like Turai where every man is glad to hear something bad about his neighbour, accusations of this sort tend to stick. A man's name can be ruined, even if the case never comes to court. Just the association with cowardice in war is a terrible taboo. Throwing away your shield is punishable by law, but the stigma is worse. It's so grave an accusation that it's rarely levelled against any of the hapless and unwilling types of men who might actually be guilty of it. Most times the commander of a cohort, faced with a soldier's cowardice, would simply beat the soldier, make sure he was full of drink when the enemy next approached, and send him back into the field. Actually taking a man to court for cowardice is the sort of thing normally reserved for politicians whose enemies are seeking a means of ruining them. Either that, or a rich man whose relatives are looking for a way to part him from his fortune. Once it's proved against you, you lose all rights as a citizen.

"Why Vadinex?" wonders Gurd.

We both know Vadinex. A huge, brutal man. An effective soldier, but dumb as an Orc; vicious and bad, even in peacetime.

"I crossed him last winter," I say. "He'd willingly play along if Rittius offered him enough."

I'm certainly not giving up my investigation on behalf of Lisutaris. Not even the King can prevent a citizen of the city walking around asking questions, though it could lead me into difficulties. I no longer have any legal status to protect my clients and could be forced by the Civil Guard to tell them everything I knew about any case I was working on. In theory anyway. In practice, the Guard can go to hell.

"Everyone can go to hell. If I run into Vadinex I still might kill him. Otherwise it's business as usual. I'm going to rescue Lisutaris. And I'm going to clear Makri. Even if I have to kill her afterwards, which I might."

"What will I do about Tanrose?"

"Go and visit her. Take flowers. Apologise for criticising her bookkeeping. And make sure Makri doesn't interfere. She's not qualified to advise normal people about how to run their lives."

"Do you think I should ask her to marry me?"

My own marriage was such a disaster, I'm loath to answer this.

"Gurd, you know I'm about as much use as a one-legged gladiator when it comes to relationships."

Unfortunately Gurd is unwilling to let me off the hook. He demands to know what I think. I seem to owe him a proper answer.

"Yes, Get married. After all, you're paying taxes. It's probably the next step."

Gurd pours himself a glass of klee. Probably he's thinking that the prospect of marriage is more frightening than facing an enemy force who outnumber you twenty to one. Which we've done, of course. More than once.

Gurd realises that he's left Makri to look after a busy tavern and goes off to assist her. Makri's coping well with the situation, aided by Dandelion, who's decided to help and is currently fumbling with a beer tap, wondering how it works. Several recently arrived regulars are looking puzzled at the sight of the bar at the Avenging Axe being run by the odd pairing of Makri and Dandelion. As a respectable local drinking establishment, the Avenging Axe doesn't generally go in for novelty attractions.

"Is this something to do with it raining frogs outside?" asks a docker, a regular customer not noted for drunkenness.

"Raining frogs?"

We all troop outside to look. It is indeed raining frogs. They bounce on the dusty road then hop off sharply. After a minute or so it stops, and the frogs disappear.

"I've never seen that before," says another dock worker.

"Yesterday I saw a unicorn," says his companion. "But I didn't like to tell anyone."

No one can explain the downpour of frogs. The general consensus is that it's a bad sign and the city is doomed, which makes for a swift rush to the bar and a lot of purchases of beer and klee. I shake my head. Unicorns, centaurs, frogs. Let someone else sort it out. I'm still livid about the accusation of cowardice. I head up to my office, ready to make someone suffer for the indignity which has been inflicted upon me. You can't expect to accuse a man like Thraxas of deserting the battlefield and not suffer some consequences. The next person who gives me so much as an unfriendly look is going to find himself at the wrong end of a hefty beating, and maybe worse.

Unfortunately, the next person I encounter is Horm the Dead, and he's not a man to whom you can just hand out a beating. He is in fact one of the most malevolent and powerful Sorcerers in the world, an insane half-Orc from the wastelands who almost destroyed the entire city a year ago. He's strong, he's evil, he hates Turai and he hates me. It's a surprise to find him sitting in my office.

"Make yourself comfortable, why don't you?" I growl at him.

Powerful Sorcerer or not, I'll have a good attempt at plunging my sword into his ribs before he can utter a spell. I demand to know what he's doing here.

Horm the Dead is a Sorcerer of striking appearance. Black clothes, pale skin, long dark hair, high cheekbones, eagle feathers in his hair and a fistful of silver rings, most of them bearing impressions of skulls. His long black cloak trails over the chair like a great pair of bat's wings.

"Are you always so uncivil to your guests?" he asks, and laughs. His laugh sounds like it comes from somewhere on the other side of the grave. The last time I heard it he was riding a dragon over the city, having just intoned a spell which drove the entire population insane. Turai would have consumed itself in a bloody orgy of fire and violence had Lisutaris, Mistress of the Sky, not managed to neutralise the spell at the very last moment. Even so, the destruction was widespread, severe enough to make Horm an eternal enemy of Turai.

"I'm famous for my incivility. Now get out of my office."

Horm ignores the suggestion.

"I am not impressed with this city," he says.

"We're not impressed with you."

"I really thought my eight-mile destruction spell would wipe you out. I was terribly disappointed when it didn't."

"So you decided to bombard us with frogs?"

"Frogs? The unusual downpour? Nothing to do with me."

Despite being half Orcish, Horm speaks very elegant Turanian. Coupled with his languid malevolence, it has an unsettling effect. As there seems to be no prospect of banishing him from my office without using violence, I ask him again why he's here.

"I thought I might hire you, Investigator. Perhaps to find a certain pendant for me?"

"I'm busy," I reply curtly, and don't let it show that I'm perturbed. With Horm the Dead now in Turai looking for the pendant, the stakes have moved up a notch, and they were already far too high.

"You know that Prince Amrag will destroy you soon?" says Horm.

I'm thrown by the sudden change of subject.

"He will?"

"Oh yes. The young Prince is proving to be a surprisingly powerful leader. He's uniting the Orcish lands. No doubt your city is already aware of this. I imagine that before too long he will be in a position to lead an army from the east."

"Then there will be a lot of dead Orcs for burning."

Horm shrugs.

"No doubt. But he'll wipe you off the map, and every other Human nation. You're not as strong as you used to be, and neither are the Elves. How strange that they should now be starting to suffer from the ravages of dwa."

Horm seems to have some very up-to-date information. It's not too many months ago that I was far down south on the Elvish Isles. It's true that dwa had found a foothold among the Elves, but I would not have thought that news of this could have travelled to the Wastelands. Unless Horm had something to do with dwa reaching the Elves in the first place. He's a user and purveyor of the drug himself, and makes money by supplying it to the Human lands, including Turai. We're all conspiring in our own downfall and seem unable to do anything about it.

"Turai has few allies. There is very little cohesion left in the League of City States. And the larger countries will look to protect their own borders. No one will help Turai when the Orcs next attack."

"Did you just come here to lecture me on politics? Because I'm a busy man."

"Of course," continues Horm, "I am not under the sway of Prince Amrag. My kingdom in the Wastelands has never been subject to rule by any of the eastern Orcish nations, and so it shall remain. But I will add my might to their forces. One gets so bored sometimes. In truth, I've been looking forward to the emergence of a new warlord."

He sits forward in his chair.

"But I digress. Turai still has a year or so left. And it also has something I want, namely the pendant."

"So you can hand it over to Prince Amrag? If you think I'd help you with that, you're madder than you look."

Horm leans forward.

"Perhaps I should just kill you now."

"Perhaps you should just bounce a spell off my fine protection charm while I stick my sword in your guts."

Horm sits back, perfectly relaxed.

"You're really not scared of me, are you? It's foolish, but admirable in a way. Tell me, why do you wish to protect this city?"

"I live here."

"You could live anywhere. Turai doesn't like you. I was concealed downstairs when that unpleasant official arrived carrying the allegation that you had once fled from the field of battle. An allegation I would judge unlikely to be true. In my kingdom I would not allow such an accusation to be made. Of course, such things are commonplace in these lands you call civilised. A true warrior will always be brought down by his cowardly enemies."

Not liking the way Horm the Dead is starting to make sense, I ask him directly about the pendant.

"What's your involvement?"

"It was offered to me for sale."

"By Sarin the Merciless?"

"Indeed."

"I seem to remember you fell out last time you worked together."

Horm waves his hand rather grandly.

"We may have argued. However, that was not the last time we worked together. Merely the last time you are aware of. Since then we have collaborated on various pieces of profitable business."

Horm smiles.

"I see that this perturbs you, Investigator. But did you really think that everything that happens around this city is known to you?"

"I know that Sarin doesn't have the pendant."

"Unfortunately she does not. Having gone to some trouble to visit this miserable city—I am of course obliged to use a variety of disguising spells—I find that the item has gone missing. The transaction was disturbed by Glixius Dragon Killer, who I look forward to removing from this world. Really, Thraxas, it has been farcical. The pendant travelling this way and that around your city, pursued here and there by either Sarin or Glixius's men, none of whom were able to resist staring into the jewel, which, of course, drove them insane. Now it is missing and whoever has the pendant seems to have hidden it very successfully. And I do so want it. As a tool for far-seeing it is quite unique, unmatched in the east or the west. Only the Elvish glass of Ruyana can compare, and the Elvish glass is, for the moment, beyond my reach."

"How did Sarin learn of its existence?"

"I have no idea," says Horm, sounding bored. "When she offered it to me for sale, I did not trouble myself with the petty details."

"Careless of you, Horm. If you'd paid attention to details you might have the pendant."

"I might. But I was not to know that Glixius Dragon Killer would become involved. I watched that rather ridiculous melee at the warehouse. The pendant was taken swiftly from the scene by a man I did not recognise. However, I traced him by sorcery and would have intercepted him last night had Glixius not interfered. By the time I had driven off Glixius, the pendant was again gone. For some reason it cannot now be located by sorcery. I am sure you will know this already."

"I'd heard. So you expect me to find it for you?"

"Why not? I will pay you a good deal more than Lisutaris, Mistress of the Sky."

Horm sneers as he pronounces her name.

"I laughed when I heard that she had been elected as head of the Sorcerers Guild. But I understand you had a hand in it. I misjudged you when we first met. You are a man of considerable competence, Thraxas."

I can't explain it, but there's something persuasive about Horm's deathly compliments. I have to throw him out before he starts winning me over.

"Perhaps," continues Horm, "you could bring me the pendant?"

"Bring it to you?"

"I would pay you very well. And though your own city

seems to place no value on your talents, my kingdom could offer you a very comfortable home . . ."

I wonder what that would be like. Thraxas, Chief Investigator of the Wastelands. It doesn't sound too bad.

"Though many of my subjects are regrettably primitive, I have a splendid palace in the mountains. Quite unassailable, and considerably better appointed than this—"

He struggles to find the right word.

"—this *place* you call home."

I look round at my office. It's very unpleasant. No place for a man to live really.

"Is it not true that the upper classes in Turai have conspired to crush you, Thraxas? Frustrated you at every turn, used their malign influence to keep you down when in reality a man of your talents should be in a position of authority high above those fools?"

"It's true."

"Not content with that, they are now assaulting the very core of your being with this outrageous accusation of cowardice. Over the years you have served this city better than any man, but will your leaders now come to your aid?"

"They won't."

There's a lot of sense in what Horm says, I slam my fist angrily on the table, raising dust.

"The Turanian aristocracy are a foul, perfidious bunch of cowards who've been conniving at my downfall from the moment I was born. Well, I've had enough!"

The inner door opens and Makri walks in. At the sight of Horm the Dead, she halts and takes out the knife she keeps concealed in her boot.

"No need to arm yourself, Makri," I say. "Horm has come to offer me a job."

"What?"

"He's on our side. We must help him to find the pendant."

"Are you crazy? Last time we met this guy he tried to kill us."

"A misunderstanding. The King is our real enemy."

Makri puts the knife back in her boot, marches straight up to me and slaps me in the face. "Slap" doesn't entirely do the blow justice. It's the sort of open-handed strike she used in the gladiatorial arena to knock the head off a troll. So fierce and unexpected is the assault that even with my considerable bulk I sag to my knees, my ears ringing and my head full of shooting stars. I look up, surprised, just in time to see Makri land another mighty blow on the other side of my face, leaving me sore, confused and generally dissatisfied with events.

"Thraxas!" yells Makri, and starts shaking me. "Don't you recognise a persuasion spell when you encounter it? You're meant to know about sorcery, for God's sake. Stop making up to this half-Orc madman and get back to being your usual oafish self."

Faced with Makri's fury, my head starts to clear. I realise that Horm was indeed using a spell of persuasion on me, one powerful enough to slowly seep past my protection charm. It's unbelievably stupid of me not to have noticed. I haul myself to my feet.

"Don't worry," I tell Makri. "I'm fine. A lesser man may have succumbed."

I turn to Horm and order him out of my office. Horm is no longer paying any attention to me. Rather he is transfixed by Makri. So transfixed that he rises from his chair, treads softly across the room then kisses her hand, something you don't often see in Twelve Seas.

"You are magnificent," he says, and stares at her.

"Don't try your persuasion spell on me," retorts Makri.

"I never imagined to meet such a woman in the west."

Makri abruptly strikes Horm in the face. So fast is her movement that Horm is lying in a heap on the floor before he knows what's happening.

I look down at him. I wish I'd done that.

Chapter Thirteen

Now I have a really powerful Sorcerer lying dazed on the floor of the office. In a few seconds he'll wake up and start destroying everything in sight.

"We have to kill him. Where's your axe?"

"I didn't bring it," says Makri.

"Why not?"

"What do you mean, why not? You're always complaining about me bringing my axe places."

"That's only when you bring it at inappropriate times. Like when I'm having a quiet beer. Right now we need it."

Makri is not satisfied with this.

"That's what you say now. But next time I walk in here with my axe I guarantee you'll start complaining again. You can't just pick and choose when a woman carries an axe, Thraxas. Either she does or she doesn't."

"I'd have thought that anyone who studied philosophy would be able to work out when was and when was not an appropriate time to be carrying heavy weapons."

Makri looks pained.

"You really shouldn't try to argue from philosophy, Thraxas. You're no good at it at all. You haven't even got a grasp of the basics. I'd say the problem lies more in the realms of your inconsistency, which, I've noticed, does tend to go up and down with your drinking."

"How did my drinking get dragged into this?"

Horm the Dead rises to his feet.

"Please stop this argument," he says. "It's making my head ache."

I point my sword at him and Makri raises her knife. Horm motions with his hand and the room cools slightly as a spell takes effect.

"Very careless of me to neglect my personal protection spell," he says, almost apologetically. "But I was not expecting to meet such a fierce warrior in this tavern. You really are magnificent."

"Stop saying that," says Makri, and shifts uncomfortably under his gaze. Makri is clad in her chainmail bikini, one of the smallest garments ever seen in the civilised world. It seems to be having an effect on Horm.

"And stop staring," says Makri.

"Forgive me."

Horm regards her for a few moments more. As a skilled practitioner of sorcery, he can learn much from the study of a person's aura.

"Orc, Elf and Human? A very rare mixture indeed. Impossible, according to some authorities. It accounts, I suppose, for your unusual rapidity of action. Though not necessarily your beauty. How can it be I have never heard of you before?"

"We did meet," answers Makri. "In the fairy glade. You were on a dragon and I killed the commander of your troops. I'd have killed you too but you flew away."

"That was you? In the heat of battle, I'm afraid I failed to register you properly. I believed you to be one of the magical characters who inhabit the glade."

He bows formally.

"Allow me to introduce myself. I am Horm the Dead, Lord of the Kingdom of Yall. And you are—?"

"Makri."

Horm raises his eyebrows.

"Makri? The champion gladiator?"

"Yes."

Horm laughs, quite heartily by his standards.

"But this is splendid. The tale of the carnage you wreaked when you escaped the slave pits is known all over the east. You killed an Orc Lord and his entire entourage in a savage fury that has become legendary. Only last month I heard a minstrel sing of it. And of course your exploits in the arena were already legendary. I am honoured to meet you."

Makri looks confused. Horm himself looks puzzled.

"How can it be that such a woman as yourself is reduced to working in a tavern?"

Not having a good answer to hand Makri remains silent, regarding Horm with suspicion, wondering if he's still trying to baffle her with a persuasion spell. As far as I can tell Horm is no longer using magic and has switched to standard flattery, something I wouldn't have guessed him to be so proficient at.

"A strange city indeed," continues Horm. "That makes the greatest swordsman it has ever seen work in a tavern."

"It's my choice."

"Come with me to my kingdom. I'll make you a general."

Makri shakes her head.

"Captain of all my armies."

I'd better interrupt before he offers her the position of Queen.

"We're not helping you find the pendant, Horm. You'd best be on your way. Sarin the Merciless is probably missing you."

"Sarin. Another interesting woman. Were I in the mood for bragging I could tell you much of value that she has brought to me from Turai and other cities, all unsuspected by your authorities.

"But," he continues, drawing his cloak around him, "I am not in the mood for bragging. I am in the mood for finding the pendant which Lisutaris, Mistress of the Sky—"

He breaks off.

"Not that she deserves such a title. Lisutaris has no great mastery over the sky. Personally I count myself as a far greater practitioner of the flying arts."

Sorcerers are always jealous of each other. I once heard Harmon Half Elf going on at length about the injustice of Tirini Snake Smiter claiming such a title when she'd never smited a snake in her life, or at the most one snake, and only a small harmless specimen at that. But Tirini is very beautiful and she'd just rejected Harmon's advances, so that probably accounts for it.

"I have a low opinion of Lisutaris," continues Horm. "Her dependence on thazis sickens me. A very poor drug for a Sorcerer."

Horm the Dead presumably regards dwa as an acceptable drug for a Sorcerer. He wouldn't be the only one.

"I have no doubt that her masked ball will be a dreary affair."

"I'm sure she hasn't invited you."

"True," admits Horm. "She has neglected to send me an invitation. But as I am already in Turai, and so adept at disguises, I am intending to attend the function. In the Wastelands, one rarely finds the opportunity to dance. I regret that you, Thraxas, are not among those deemed worthy to attend."

I don't catch any flicker of emotion on Makri's face but Horm does.

"You are going? Excellent. Perhaps we may converse more regarding my offer of employment."

He turns to me.

"I see that you have nothing to tell me regarding the pendant, so I will now depart. I had intended to kill you, because I've always resented the role you played in the failure of my spell to destroy this city. I worked long and hard on that incantation. But I have now changed my mind. I do not wish to do anything that may upset your companion Makri, who I judge to be the finest flower in all of Turai."

He studies her for a while more.

"Your hair. So extremely luxurious yet not sorcerously enhanced. I have never seen its like. Who, may I ask, were your parents?"

Makri's face sets into an expression of malign hostility and she raises her knife a fraction.

"Forgive me," says Horm. "I did not mean to intrude. Thraxas, we shall no doubt meet again. Till then, farewell."

Horm steps lightly towards the outside door, but he hasn't finished yet. He pauses and turns his head, causing his long dark hair to sway quite dramatically. He may have worked on the effect.

"Your trouble at the College. Have you looked into the role of Barius?"

"Barius. Professor Toarius's son. I was about to look for

him before I was interrupted by Consul Kalius. What about him?"

"A dwa addict. So I understand from my business contacts."

Horm makes a formal little bow, then slips quietly out of the door.

"That was unexpected," says Makri.

"It was. At least he didn't destroy my room this time."

"Shouldn't we follow him?" asks Makri, eager for action.

"I can't believe he's going to Lisutaris's ball. Everyone is going except me."

"Stop complaining about the ball, Thraxas. We have to get busy."

I hunt around for a beer.

"It's just so annoying. Horm's going. Cicerius is going. You're going."

I stare at Makri balefully.

"I mean, what did you really do for Lisutaris? All right, you were her bodyguard, but who did all the work? Me. She would never have been elected head of the Sorcerers Guild without me."

I take a heavy slug of beer. Makri is regarding me with a curious expression.

"Thraxas. Every time I think I've discovered the true shallowness of your character, you manage to surprise me with some further outrageous lack of depth. Have you forgotten what's going on around you? Lisutaris is missing one important pendant and most of the bad guys in the world are after it at this moment, including several powerful Sorcerers and a killer who once put a crossbow bolt through my chest. Not only is this bad for Turai, it's also bad for your client, because Kalius will be down on her like a bad spell when he gets proof of the loss, if he doesn't have that already. Apart from this, I've been expelled from college and you've sworn to put that right, and apart from that, you've been accused of cowardice at a battle that took place seventeen years ago and are consequently no longer allowed to investigate pending a Senate inquiry. Also, it's raining frogs."

"I am aware of these matters."

"Then stop whining on about Lisutaris's masked ball like a spoiled young princess and do some investigating."

I sit down at my desk and drag a new bottle of beer from the drawer.

"I thought I'd just drink some beer instead. You investigate. Finest flower in Turai indeed. After you've investigated you can go and be Captain of Horm's armies. Have a good time."

"It couldn't be worse than listening to you."

"Maybe not. But if he tries to make you his bride, watch out. You might have to be dead first."

"What do you mean?" says Makri, curiously.

"Horm the Dead is rumoured to actually have been dead. Died by his own hand then returned from the grave in some evil ritual known only to himself."

"Why would anyone do that?" wonders Makri.

"Presumably the death-ritual gave him unearthly powers. I don't know if any of it's really true. He might just be pretend-ing to have been dead to impress people."

"He does look very pale," says Makri.

"Not too pale to clutter up my office and go around kissing people's hands."

"Thraxas, that barely makes sense."

"Not too pale to go to Lisutaris's ball and spend the night dancing with a bunch of senators who've never done an honest day's work in their lives."

Makri wonders out loud at my intransigence and stupidity. I continue to drink beer. After a while she departs.

It's hot as Orcish hell in here. I detest this city and everyone in it. It's intensely annoying the way everyone is always playing up to Makri. The finest flower in Turai! It's ridiculous. An Orcish savage in a ludicrous bikini more like. Unable to find any more beer in my desk, I go through to my only other room and hunt under the bed for my emergency supply.

Chapter Fourteen

The city is full of mythical creatures and dead Humans.
Reports from all sides indicate an unexplained outbreak
of unicorns, centaurs, naiads, dryads and mermaids. No
harm is caused by these creatures—they tend to vanish when
pursued—but it makes the population edgy. The thought of
Orcish invasion is never far below the conscious thoughts of
the citizenry, and anything strange or unexplained tends to
be thought of as an evil portent.

I've been chasing round the city looking for a powerful
sorcerous item. Strange sorcerous events are now happening. It
doesn't take a genius to think they might be connected, but if
they are, no one knows why, not even Lisutaris. Furthermore,
there seem to be too many of these occurrences for them all

to be linked to one missing green jewel, even if the green jewel could produce these events, which it can't.

As for the dead Humans, it's another epidemic. Everywhere the authorities look, they find another group of corpses. Some with wounds, some just dead for no apparent reason. Again, it's hard to link this exactly to the missing pendant. At the exact same time as three market workers are found dead in the centre of town, four aqueduct maintenance men are found slaughtered in Pashish. Lisutaris's pendant can't be causing it all, and in a city where death is a common occurrence, it's impossible to work out which of the fatalities might be linked to the pendant.

After waking with a headache, and visiting the public baths to cleanse myself of the accumulated filth of several days' activity in hot weather, I go to see Cicerius at the Abode of Justice. He's already aware of the charge which has been laid against me.

"I don't sympathise in the slightest," he says.

"Thanks for your support."

"You were clearly warned that trouble would arise from your use of the Tribunate powers."

"But I did it anyway. And now I'm in trouble."

"You are, though personally I do not believe the charge of throwing away your shield and fleeing the battlefield," says Cicerius. "I studied your record quite carefully before I first hired you to work for me. As I recall, you were an insubordinate soldier but your valour was never questioned. But I cannot have the charge dropped. The matter must go before a Senate committee, and until then your Tribune's powers are revoked, as is your investigating licence."

"Can't you use your influence? My accuser is Vadinex and he works for Praetor Capatius."

Cicerius knows Capatius very well. Not only is the Praetor

the richest man in the city, he's a senior member of the Traditionals, Cicerius's party.

"Last year I got in Capatius's way and now he's getting his revenge. Can't you get him off my back?"

The Deputy Consul is unenthusiastic, though he knows I'm speaking the truth when I claim he owes me a favour.

"Were you with Vadinex at the Battle of Sanasa?"

"We were in the same regiment. I don't remember ever being close to him on the battlefield. But I was with plenty of other men who are still alive today who'll testify on my behalf."

"So you hope, Thraxas. My experience as a lawyer has taught me that men's memories can be strangely affected by the passage of seventeen years. And they can be affected a good deal more by bribery. A charge of this sort, brought after so many years, will not be easy to defend in court if your opponents have planned it well."

Cicerius muses for a while.

"I really doubt that Capatius is behind this charge."

"He has to be. Vadinex is his man."

"Even so, I doubt it. It is true that you inconvenienced Praetor Capatius last year, but the inconvenience was minor by his standards. A mere blip in his considerable income. I have seen the Praetor many times since then and he has never given me the impression that he holds any strong grudge against you. I am aware that you do not trust him, but I believe him to be far more honest than you give him credit for. Like many rich men, he has suffered at the hands of the Populares, who are always keen to accuse any worthy supporter of the King of corruption. Capatius himself fought bravely in the war, with a cohort he raised and equipped at his own expense. In my experience, it is rare for a man who fought in that campaign to raise a false charge against another who also fought. It would go against his sense of military honour."

I'm not convinced. Capatius is obscenely wealthy. I can't believe anyone could get to be so rich and still have a sense of honour.

"You offended many people when you prevented a full investigation of Lisutaris's actions at the warehouse," points out the Deputy Consul. "Far more likely that one of them would now wish to see you punished. Rittius, for instance. The head of Palace Security has long disliked you."

"Yes, it's possible it's Rittius. But my instinct tells me that Capatius has put Vadinex up to it. So I appeal to you to make efforts on my behalf. Because as you will understand, Deputy Consul, if I'm dragged before a Senate committee on a charge of cowardice, I'll be obliged to kill my accuser and flee the city."

Cicerius looks shocked.

"You will obey the law of Turai," he informs me sternly.

"Absolutely."

"While you are here," says Cicerius, "would you care to tell me the precise nature of the difficulties that Lisutaris finds herself in?"

"No real difficulties, Deputy Consul. A minor matter of a missing diary."

I intimate that I am unable to say more due to Investigator-client privilege.

"You have no such privileges. Your licence has been suspended."

"Then I've suffered a sudden loss of memory."

"Yesterday a unicorn wandered through the Senate while I was speaking," says Cicerius.

"That must have livened things up."

"My speech did not need to be livened up. It was already quite lively enough. Do you have any idea why these creatures should suddenly be infesting the city?"

"None at all."

"Nothing to do with our powerful Sorceress Lisutaris?"

"Not as far as I know."

Cicerius dismisses me. I'm fairly satisfied with the meeting. He might help. If nothing else, I've ascended the social ladder a fraction in the last year. Not too long ago I'd never have been granted permission to see the Deputy Consul, never mind ask him for a favour.

Halfway between Cicerius's office and the outskirts of Thamlin, I encounter a figure walking briskly up the road in a cloak and hood which hides her features.

"Makri? What are you doing here?"

Makri pulls back her hood a little.

"I'm in disguise."

"I can see that. Why?"

"I'm going to kill Vadinex."

"What? Why?"

Makri shrugs.

"I thought I'd help you."

"How were you going to find him?"

"Call in at Praetor Capatius's mansion and find out from someone there where he was likely to be."

"And then go and kill him?"

"That's right. If he was dead, there wouldn't be a charge against you, would there?"

I'm almost touched by Makri's concern.

"It's not a bad plan. But I've just asked the Deputy Consul to intervene on my behalf and I don't want to offend him by killing Vadinex before it's absolutely necessary."

Makri shrugs. She hasn't asked me a single question about the Battle of Sanasa because, I know, she does not regard it as possible that I fled the field. I remember that I'm friends with Makri and feel bad about giving her a hard time.

"I'm about to hunt through some taverns in Kushni for Barius, Professor Toarius's son. I think that if we apply some pressure we might get to the bottom of this theft at the college."

Makri wants to come along, so we set off towards the centre of the city.

"Was it a really bad disguise?" asks Makri.

"Not too bad. But I recognised your walk."

"I didn't really need a disguise at all, but I thought if I killed Vadinex it would be better if people didn't know it was me that did it. You know, with us living in the same tavern. It might have cast suspicion on you."

"I appreciate you making the effort. I'm sorry I moaned at you."

"It was more than moaning. It was vilification and character assassination."

"Surely not."

"You called me a vile Orcish wench."

"Then I apologise for any offence. As always, I meant it in a positive sense."

The heat is stifling. Makri removes her cloak as we walk through the dusty streets.

"I did mess things up with Tanrose. When I suggested she take some time to think about her feelings, I wasn't expecting her to leave the tavern."

"It's not really your fault, Makri. The problem is with Gurd. He's been a bachelor so long, he's scared to acknowledge any sort of affection for her. That's why he started criticising her bookkeeping."

"To disguise his affection?"

"Yes."

Makri nods.

"I have encountered this sort of thing in the plays of the

Elvish bard Las-ar-Heth. Not concerning bookkeeping, but similar. The great Elvish lord Avenath-ir-Yill once made his queen cry by accusing her of infidelity with a unicorn, but really he was just upset because she no longer played the harp to him at bedtime. The reason for this was that her hands were sore from plaiting the unicorn's mane, which she had to do to keep her son alive, but of course she couldn't explain this to her husband without letting him know about the curse which hung over her family."

My head is starting to spin.

"This is similar to Gurd and Tanrose?"

"Very. A frank exchange of views would have resolved the problem, but they both had secrets they didn't want to reveal. Eventually, of course, it led to the great schism between the tribes of Yill and Evena, which, I understand, is not fully resolved even now."

"You read all this in a play?"

Makri nods. She is apparently a great enthusiast for the plays of the Elvish bard Las-ar-Heth.

"Quite an unconventional rhyme scheme, and rather archaic in tone, but very stirring."

"I'll read some at the first opportunity," I say, which makes Makri laugh, which she doesn't do that often.

"Is that a mermaid in that fountain?"

We stare across the road at the large fountain. Sitting at the feet of the statue of St. Quatinius there is indeed a mermaid. Children laugh, and point. The mermaid smiles seductively, then fades away.

"Turai is becoming a very interesting place. Are we all going mad?"

"I don't know. At least it's only friendly creatures who've been appearing. It's not going to be much fun if dragons start roaming the streets."

"I liked the frogs," says Makri.

By this time we're passing through the royal market, just north of Kushni, one of Turai's main concentrations of goods for sale. The shops here sell clothes, jewellery, wine, weapons, expensive goods mainly. The market stalls sell foodstuffs but are very different from the cheap markets of Twelve Seas. Here the servants of the rich come to order household provisions from market traders whose stalls are full of the highest-quality fare, often imported from the nations to the west, or even the Elvish Isles.

Makri stares through the window of a jeweller's shop.

"Who earns enough to buy these things?" she wonders out loud.

A young woman emerges from the shop, followed by two servants. When she sees Makri she gives her the slightest of nods before passing by. I ask Makri who the young woman was.

"Avenaris. Lisutaris's secretary."

I'm already in pursuit. I've been forbidden to question this young woman. Always makes an Investigator suspicious. I cut her off with my bulk. She regards me rather nervously. I introduce myself but she already knows who I am.

"I was wondering if you could help me with a few questions."

"Lisutaris would not wish me to talk about her business with anyone," says Avenaris. "Even an Investigator she hired. Excuse me."

She tries to walk past. I get in the way. She's looking very, very nervous. More nervous than she should be. I'm not that frightening, not in daylight anyway. Not frightening enough to make a person develop a facial tic within seconds of meeting me, yet Avenaris's eyelid is starting to tremble violently.

"Maybe you could just tell me a little about what happened that day at the stadium—"

"What is going on here?"

It's Lisutaris, Mistress of the Sky.

"Did I not specifically tell you to leave my secretary alone?"

"He stood in my way," says Avenaris, making it sound like a major crime. She's now close to tears.

"I'm sorry," says Lisutaris, attempting to pacify her. "He really had no business bothering you. Go home now, I'll make sure he doesn't trouble you again."

Avenaris walks off swiftly, still attended by the servants. The Sorceress regards me with fury.

"How dare you harass my staff!"

"Save the lecture, Lisutaris. What's the matter with her? I asked her a polite question and she practically broke down in tears."

"She is a young woman of nervous disposition. Far too delicate to be confronted by the likes of you. I must insist—"

"You should've let me talk to her. I get the strong impression she knows something."

"Do I have to remind you that Avenaris is my niece? I did not hire you to harass my family. For the last time, stay away from my secretary."

Lisutaris looks genuinely threatening. I drop the subject, for now anyway. I'll pursue it later, no matter what Lisutaris says.

"Encountered any unicorns?" I ask.

"No. But there were two mermaids in my fish ponds, albeit briefly. I'm baffled. They're obviously sorcerous apparitions but I can't trace their source."

"Did you get my message about Horm the Dead?"

Lisutaris nods, and frowns.

"Horm the Dead is a very dangerous individual. Consul Kalius should be immediately informed that he is in the city."

"And has he been?"

"No," admits Lisutaris. "I'm still trying to keep things quiet."

In the past few days Lisutaris has been subjected to much questioning from fellow Sorcerers and government officials. So far it has remained informal.

"Deputy Consul Cicerius visited to ask me about some aqueduct renovations. I wasn't aware that he valued my opinion on the city's water supply. Harmon Half Elf happened to find himself in the vicinity and dropped in to share an amusing story about some Elvish Sorcerers."

Given Lisutaris's status, it's difficult for anyone to come right out and demand to know what's going on, though it's perfectly obvious that something is. However, having moved heaven, earth and the three moons to get her elected as head of the Sorcerers Guild, no one in Turai wants her to be plunged into disgrace only a few months later. Turai would be severely damaged in the eyes of all nations.

"They're hovering round the subject. I've been keeping quiet like you suggested, but I can't hold out for ever. Tilupasis was sniffing round for information and you know what a cunning operator she is. I was reduced to telling her that I really had to ask her to leave because I needed some privacy to smoke my thazis pipe, so there goes my reputation among Turai's aristocratic matrons. Now it'll be all over Thamlin that Lisutaris can't grant you more than a half-hour audience before she has to smoke thazis."

"Didn't everyone know that already?" asks Makri, who has not yet learned how to be tactful.

"I am not reliant on thazis," says Lisutaris, coldly.

"Oh," says Makri. "Sorry. I thought you were. I remember when you collapsed at the Sorcerers Assemblage and I had to carry you to your pipe and you were gasping about how you needed thazis, so I just naturally assumed—"

"Could we discuss this another time?" says Lisutaris, shooting her an angry glance. She turns the angry glance in my direction.

"Not that I had much reputation left after word got around that I'd hired you to buy back my diary which I was desperate to retrieve due to its being full of extremely intimate love poems. I understand that guessing the identity of my secret lover is now a popular game at dinner parties."

"I'm shocked, Lisutaris. When I told Kalius about your diary, I thought he'd keep it a secret."

"Who is it?" asks Makri.

"Who is who?"

"The person you're in love with?"

"I'm not in love with anyone. Thraxas made it up."

Makri looks puzzled.

"Why?"

"I needed a cover story. It was all I could think of."

Makri is of the opinion that I could have done better.

"After all, many people say you're one of the finest liars in the city."

Lisutaris is certain that the Consul is going to ask to see the pendant when he comes to the ball.

"Kalius might not be sharp as an Elf's ear, but even he must know by now I've lost the pendant. Damn it, I wish I hadn't chosen this moment to hold a social function."

"Talking of your social function," I say, "Horm the Dead mentioned that he might be paying a visit."

"Really?"

"Yes. And as you say, Horm is a very dangerous individual. I think it would be wise for you to have some extra personal protection at the ball."

"You may be right," says Lisutaris.

I wait for my invitation. Lisutaris turns to Makri.

"Would you mind being my bodyguard again?"

"I'd be delighted," answers Makri.

I stare morosely at the jeweller's window. Lisutaris is a disgrace to the city. Her abuse of thazis is a public scandal. She deserves to be exiled.

"What do you suggest we do now, Investigator?"

"I've no idea."

"I can't really blame you for that," sighs Lisutaris. "I have no idea what to do either."

I've started to believe that there is no point investigating. Either someone is deliberately leading us on and mocking us at every turn, or the situation has become so chaotic that there is no point in doing anything. Either way, I'm beaten.

"If no one has any plans for saving the city, how about going to see Barius?" suggests Makri, brightly.

"Who is Barius?" asks Lisutaris.

"Professor Toarius's son. I think he might be able to shed some light on Makri's expulsion."

Lisutaris offers to take us there in her carriage, which is waiting nearby. She doesn't feel like going home, fearing that she will once more be confronted by an inquisitive Sorcerer or curious government official.

"Six more deaths in the city today," I say. "Brings the total to twenty-seven, near as I can count. For that many unexplained deaths the Abode of Justice will call in a Sorcerer. Old Hasius the Brilliant will learn every detail of the affair."

"Not for a long time," says Lisutaris. "The moons are way out of conjunction."

For a Sorcerer to look back in time, it's necessary for the three moons to be in a particular alignment. According to Lisutaris, we're in the middle of one of the longest blank periods of the decade. I'd have known that if I wasn't so lousy at sorcery.

"It'll be months before Sorcerers can look back in time. If that wasn't the case I'd have been looking back myself."

The carriage takes us towards Kushni. The driver shouts at some revellers who are blocking the street. They look like they might be inclined to argue over right of way, but when they recognise Lisutaris's rainbow livery on the side of the carriage, they hastily move, not wishing to be blasted by a spell.

"Do you think we should revise our bet?" asks Makri. "The three of us have ended up placing a bet on thirty-five deaths. But with the count now at twenty-seven this may not be high enough."

Lisutaris manages a grim laugh.

"True. And if the Consul freezes my assets before bringing me to trial, I may be in need of some money to pay for a lawyer. What's the cut-off point for this wager?"

Makri looks a little uncomfortable.

"Well, you know, when the case comes to an end . . ."

"And when would that be?"

"When Thraxas solves it. Or gets killed. Or you get arrested."

Lisutaris is shocked.

"The Turanian masses are gambling on me being arrested?"

"Only tangentially," says Makri.

"Have they no respect for the head of the Sorcerers Guild?"

"Don't complain," I tell the Sorcerer. "It's not as bad as betting on me dying."

"I think Lisutaris dying also brings the betting to an end," says Makri, helpfully. "But no one is really expecting that to happen. Apart from Parax the shoemaker; I think he wagered a little on Lisutaris's death. And maybe one or two others. Captain Rallee as well. But not many. It's definitely not as popular an option as Thraxas handing in his toga. Do you have any thazis?"

We smoke Lisutaris's thazis sticks as we make our way through the busy streets. Even in the tense situation I appreciate the high quality of her narcotic.

"Grown in your own gardens?"

"Yes. Or rather, in the glasshouse I built last year."

"You have a glasshouse?"

"A special construction," explains the Sorcerer. "For protecting plants from the elements and maximising the sunlight that feeds them. They were first used in Simnia. I believe mine is the first in Turai."

I've never heard of such a thing, and once more marvel at Lisutaris's dedication to her favourite substance. Thazis is imported into Turai from the southeast, where it's extensively cultivated. Though I've known people to occasionally produce their own plants, I don't think anyone else in the city is capable of growing it in volume. A glasshouse. I would hardly have believed it was possible. It must have been extremely expensive.

"Fabulously expensive," agrees Lisutaris. "But with the amount of rain we have in Turai, nothing else will do."

Lisutaris turns sharply to Makri.

"Why has Captain Rallee placed a bet on me dying?" she demands. "Has he some inside information?"

Makri doesn't think so, but Lisutaris is troubled. Maybe it's the thazis. Overuse can lead to feelings of paranoia. I ask Makri casually if many people are betting money on me dying.

"Hundreds of people," answers Makri. "It's a strong favourite. The moment the Brotherhood got involved, money started pouring in."

"I'm damned if I'm going to die just to win money for a lot of degenerates in the Avenging Axe. You think the Brotherhood worries me? Anyway, I thought this betting was just on the body count?"

Makri shrugs.

"It sort of grew. Moxalan was getting so many enquiries he had to take on an assistant and widen his range."

The carriage pulls up and we climb out into the dusty street. Lisutaris is clad in her rainbow cloak. Possibly fatalistic by now, she makes no attempt to disguise herself as we stride into the Rampant Unicorn, a tavern on the outskirts of Kushni where, I'm told, Barius is often to be found. It's yet another appalling den of iniquity, and at the sight of the head of the Sorcerers Guild striding through the doors, the place goes quiet. Several customers, presuming that Lisutaris must be here on official business, and whatever this business is it can't be good for them, scurry for cover as the Mistress of the Sky heads towards the bar.

"I am looking for a young man by the name of Barius," she says.

"He's upstairs," blurts the barman, quaking as he imagines the effect a spell from a disgruntled Sorcerer might have on him.

"This way," says Lisutaris, leading myself and Makri up the stairs. She's looking pleased with herself.

"I have never investigated anything before. It does not seem to be overly difficult."

I stifle a sarcastic response, and follow Lisutaris to one of four doors that lead off the upstairs corridor. Lisutaris tries the first door. Finding it locked, she mutters a minor word of power and it springs open. Inside the private room we find a stout man in a toga in the embrace of a woman who's young enough to be his granddaughter, but probably isn't a relation.

"I beg your pardon, Senator Alesius," says Lisutaris grandly, and leads us back into the corridor.

"Well, that spoiled his afternoon's entertainment," I say. "The thing about investigating, you don't just barge through the first door you come to."

"And how did you expect me to choose?"

"It's a matter of experience and intuition," I explain. "You develop it after a few years in the business."

"Very well," says Lisutaris, motioning to the three remaining doors. "Which do you recommend?"

I select the door on the left. Lisutaris again mutters a word of power and it springs open. Inside we find a well-dressed middle-aged woman with plenty of jewels and a younger man, naked, who looks like he might be a professional athlete, both of them very busy with a pipe full of dwa.

"I beg your pardon, Marwini," says Lisutaris, and withdraws from the room, quite elegantly. Makri and I stumble out after her, rather embarrassed at the whole thing.

"Who was that?"

"Praetor Capatius's wife," says Lisutaris. "Really, I had no idea. One always understood that they were a contented couple. Only last week she informed me over a glass of wine that she had never felt happier with her husband."

"Probably because he's coming home less."

"Is this sort of behaviour standard all over Kushni?"

"Pretty standard," I reply. "Though they might have to find a new place to misbehave if you keep using spells to open doors."

"I want to pick the next room," says Makri.

Inside the next room we find Barius. He's lying semiconscious on a couch. The room stinks of dwa. From the overpowering aroma and general squalidness of the situation, I'd say he'd been lying here for a few days.

"I picked the right room," says Makri, happily.

"You only had two doors to choose from."

"That's not the point. You were wrong and I was right."

"It's completely the point. The odds were entirely different."

"Do you two never stop bickering?" says Lisutaris. "Here is your suspect. What do you do now?"

"Waken him up, if that's possible."

There's a pitcher of stale water beside the couch. I take a lesada leaf from the small bag on my belt and try getting Barius to swallow it. It's a difficult process and I'm careful in case Barius chooses this moment to vomit. Finally I succeed in making him swallow the leaf.

"Now we wait. Lisutaris, please lock the door again."

Elvish lesada leaves are extremely efficient in cleansing the system of any noxious substances. They're hard to get hold of in the Human lands and normally I'd be reluctant to waste one on a dwa addict who's only going to fill himself full of dwa again at the first opportunity, but I don't have time to wait for Barius to come round naturally. A few minutes after he's swallowed the leaf, the colour is returning to his skin and his pupils are reverting to their normal size. He coughs, and struggles to rise. I give him more water.

"Who are you?"

"Thraxas. Investigator."

"Investigator . . . from Ve . . . Vee . . ." he gasps.

"No. Not from the Venarius Agency. I'm independent and I can help you."

"What do you want?"

"I want to ask you a few questions."

Possibly the lesada leaf has done its job too well. Barius has regained some youthful vigour and defiance.

"Go to hell," he says, and struggles to rise from the couch. I place my arm on his shoulder and hold him down. Makri is by my side. I can sense her impatience. If Barius has any information that can help to clear her name, she's not going to let him leave the room without imparting it. Lisutaris meanwhile looks bored, and in the sordid, foul-smelling room, less like she's having a good time.

I ask Barius if he knew about the theft of the money at the Guild College. He gives an impression of a young man too confused by dwa addiction to know much about anything. I'm about to make some threats about telling his father and all his snooty relatives just what he gets up to in his spare time when Makri's patience snaps.

Makri has two swords with her, one Elvish and gleaming and one Orcish and dark. She brought the Orcish blade from the gladiator pits and received the Elvish sword as a gift from the Elves on Avula. Both fine weapons, as fine as any held by anyone in Turai. Either one would fetch enough at auction to pay for Makri's classes for a year or more, but Makri will never sell a weapon. She draws both of her swords. The light from the torch on the wall reflects brightly off the Elvish blade, but the Orcish sword seems to absorb light. It's a vile weapon, and caused great offence to the Elves when Makri took it to their islands. Makri deftly positions the black Orcish sword under Barius's chin.

"Tell us about the money or I'll kill you right now," she says.

Barius realises she's serious. He looks at me fearfully, waiting for me to protect him. I look up at the ceiling. Makri pushes her sword forward. A trickle of blood appears on Barius's throat. Barius cringes backwards, then tries to shrug as if unconcerned.

"So I took five gurans from a locker. Who cares?"

"I do, you cusux," says Makri, raising her sword. "For the price of a shot of dwa, you'd ruin my life?"

I raise my hand to block Makri's arm.

"It's okay, we've got what we came for. We can go."

"*Have* you got what you came for?" enquires Lisutaris. "Will such a confession under duress stand up in court?"

"There isn't going to be any court case. Professor Toarius is going to quietly reinstate Makri when I tell him that his son stole the money for dwa and I have witnesses to that effect. The Professor is of course very keen to protect the family name, which is no doubt why he was so quick to pin the rap on Makri in the first place."

Barius is shaking. I place my arm round him and lower him back on to the couch. He can sleep it off. Then he should go home, but I doubt he will. It's not my problem. I'm concerned to learn that the Venarius Investigation Agency has already got to him. I still don't know who hired them. Outside the Rampant Unicorn, Lisutaris shudders, rather delicately.

"What a disgusting place. I am astonished that Marwini should choose to have an assignation in such a location. Who on earth was that naked young man?"

"One of the King's athletes, I think. On his way up in the world. Or down, maybe, if Praetor Capatius catches him."

"It's all rather embarrassing," says Lisutaris. "Marwini is one of my guests at the ball tomorrow. As is Senator Alesius. I am not so surprised to find him here, of course. His behaviour is well known in certain circles."

"So can I do my examination now?" says Makri.

"I'll see Toarius tomorrow. It'll be fine."

"When is this examination?" asks Lisutaris.

"The day after tomorrow."

"So soon? Will you still be able to attend my ball as my bodyguard?"

"Of course," says Makri. "I've already completed my studies. But did I tell you I have to stand up and speak to the whole class? It's really stressful."

Makri is still complaining as we climb into Lisutaris's carriage. One problem solved, more or less. Now we only have the matter of an important pendant to find, followed by Thraxas being hauled before a Senate committee on an allegation of cowardice. Somehow I can't concentrate. It's just so annoying the way Lisutaris, the so-called Mistress of the Sky, flatly refuses to invite me to her masked ball. I suppose it's only to be expected. The upper classes of Turai are notorious for their degeneracy and ingratitude. Adultery. Dwa. Corruption. All manner of disgusting behaviour. An honest working man like myself is far better off not associating with them.

Chapter Fifteen

At the Avenging Axe there's a summons waiting ordering me to report to the Consul, and another message, from Harmon Half Elf, requesting a meeting. I throw both messages in the bin and head downstairs for a beer. There I find Dandelion behind the bar being irritating, Gurd still looking as miserable as a Niojan whore, no food on offer, and a great cluster of dock workers all keen to know if there have been any more deaths recently. The front door opens. A government official in a toga walks in, swiftly followed by another official in a toga, and they each beat a path towards me, bearing scrolls.

The togas are hitting the Avenging Axe thick and fast these days. It's a while since I've worn one. I used to when

I worked at the Palace, for official duties. They're expensive garments. Quite awkward to wear, but it lets everyone know you're not the sort of person who wastes his time doing manual labour.

"Rittius, head of Palace Security, commands that you visit him immediately," says the first official. "To discuss important matters of state."

"The senate licensing committee, finding you in violation of an order prohibiting you from investigating, requires you to attend a—"

"I'll be right there," I say, finishing my beer in one swift gulp. "I just have to change my boots."

I only have one pair of boots. They're not to know that. Once in my office I head straight for the door and down the outside stairs, pausing only to mutter the minor incantation I use for a locking spell.

The two rival vendors have now come to blows. I use my body weight to send them flying in opposite directions and start walking swiftly, heading for anywhere that is free of summonses, enquiries and any other oppressive state instruments.

The situation is now disastrous. I have abandoned all hope of successfully bringing matters to a conclusion. Clearly Lisutaris is going to be unmasked at her own masked ball, revealed to the world as a useless incompetent who's lost the pendant, thereby severely endangering Turai. This will swiftly be followed by a general round-up of all guilty parties, which will certainly include me. I'm going to be charged with failing to report a crime, obstructing the authorities, lying to the Consul, going against the wishes of the Senate and God knows what else. Even the claim of Investigator-client confidentiality—dubious at best in matters of national security—won't do me any good, because I've been stripped of my licence and can no longer claim to be an Investigator in the legal sense of the word.

My most likely destination is a prison ship. Maybe even a slave galley.

I strain to think of some way out of the dire situation. A golden tree erupts from the road in front of me and stands there looking pretty. This is now becoming seriously disconcerting. There's a time and a place for sorcery and it's not in the middle of Quintessence Street while I'm trying to concentrate. Attractive as the tree is, no one is pleased to see it. Onlookers mutter alarming comments about portents for the destruction of the city and the more nervous among them start wailing and kneeling down to pray.

I have some experience of this sort of thing. In the magic space, a kind of sorcerous dimension to which only those with magical powers have access, things appear and disappear all the time. When it's flowers and unicorns it's fine, but last time I was there a volcano erupted and I was lucky to escape with my life. If the magic space is somehow breaking through into Turai—which is impossible, but I can't think of any other explanation—then it might well mean the destruction of the city. Now I think about it, it might mean the destruction of everything. The tree disappears as swiftly as it arrived. Trusting that the Sorcerers Guild is currently working on the strange apparitions, I get back to my own problems.

I could go to Kalius and tell him everything I know, but it might be too late for that. Once Kalius learns I've known about the missing jewel for a week, he'll be down on me like a bad spell. I'll be turned over to Palace Security and Rittius will positively dance with glee as he's locking me up. So telling the truth seems to be out of the question. Unfortunately, keeping silent doesn't hold out much hope either. Everything is going to come out at the ball tomorrow.

I wonder if it might profit me to actually find out how the pendant went missing in the first place. Lisutaris has consistently prevented me from properly investigating this, claiming that only the recovery of the pendant is important. Maybe if I actually turned up at the Consul's office with full details of who took the pendant and why, I might be able to bargain for a lesser sentence. It goes against the grain, though. I'd be acting against my client's wishes. I keep this in reserve, though it's a weak plan at best.

The only thing which would really help would be if I found the pendant right now and returned it to Lisutaris. She could present it to Consul Kalius and then just clam up about everything. Completely deny that it had ever been missing. Who could prove her wrong? It might still get us off the hook.

It strikes me that I may have been mistaken in following Lisutaris's so-called leads all around the city. Naturally, when a man is looking for a lost pendant and the head of the Sorcerers Guild arrives in a hurry and tells him she has located said pendant, the man goes along with it. But where has it got me? Precisely nowhere. A lot of dead bodies and a headache from rushing around in the heat. For all I know the jewel might never have even been in any of these locations. Someone could have been leading Lisutaris on. Just because Lisutaris is extremely powerful it doesn't mean she's always right. Maybe if I'd just stuck to my own methods of investigation I might have made better progress. I've solved a lot of crimes by trudging round the city asking questions.

By this time I've walked clear down to the southern wall of the city. I pass through a small gate that leads on to the shore, a rocky stretch of coastline some way from the harbour. Further along the coast there are some stretches of golden sands, but this close to the city the sea washes up against a barren patch of rocky pools. The area stinks from the sewage which flows out of Turai, making it a place which few people visit. Even the fishermen who take crabs from the pools tend to stay clear of this polluted part of the landscape, particularly in the heat of summer. The offensive odour makes me wrinkle my nose. I wonder why I've walked here. I should have made for the harbour and checked out the ships. I might have found a trireme heading south and asked for passage.

I spot a figure in the distance, half hidden behind a tall spur of rock. I'm about to leave when something about his movements strikes me as familiar. My curiosity piqued, I stroll over, taking care not to slip on the slime that clings to the rocks. When I reach the spur I find Horm the Dead scrabbling around in a small pool.

"Looking for crabs?"

He looks up, surprised at the interruption.

"I sent the pendant here for safekeeping after I took it from Glixius," he announces. "But it's gone."

Before I can deny any involvement, Horm states that he already knows I haven't taken it.

"I've long since stopped worrying about your investigative powers. It is part of your fate to always be too late. But who can have found the pendant here?"

Horm withdraws his hand from the water, shaking off the dark liquid with some disgust.

"It really is too bad," he proclaims. "I am now heartily sick of this whole affair."

"Everyone is sick of it."

"And yet I must have the pendant."

"Why not give it up?" I suggest. "You probably don't really need it."

"I am afraid I do," says Horm. Unexpectedly he smiles. "I have promised it to Prince Amrag. Rash perhaps, but true. Our new Orcish warlord seems to have taken offence at some comments I made that were reported to him by his spies. Comments which were taken out of context, of course . . . Still . . . I really must have the pendant."

"You mean your neck is in danger if you don't deliver the goods?"

"I would not go as far as that," says Horm. "But it will certainly help to smooth out the misunderstanding."

I'm gathering from this that Horm the Dead has managed to get himself quite seriously on the wrong side of Prince Amrag. A sorcerous lord like Horm doesn't go around dipping his hands into polluted pools of water unless he has a lot of smoothing-over to do.

"Yes, Horm, it's a problem. You offend someone in authority and they make your life hell. Happens to me all the time."

"Prince Amrag has no authority over me."

"True. But he's soon going to have the biggest army in the east."

We walk up the beach together. By his standards Horm the Dead is being positively convivial, and he's not even using a spell of persuasion. He simply regards me as so little threat he is unconcerned about how much I know of his affairs. In fact he seems eager to discuss them.

"I presume, as you are still wandering vacantly around the city, that Lisutaris has not recovered the pendant?"

"Not to my knowledge."

"And Glixius Dragon Killer certainly does not have it. As for the criminal gangs of Turai, I feel that neither of them has it either. I have enough contacts in your Turanian underworld to have learned by now if they had. Do you think your Turanian Sorcerers Guild might have recovered the green jewel?"

I shrug. I've no idea.

"I find this all very unsatisfactory," complains the Sorcerer. "In a matter such as this I would have expected a little discretion.

In some ways it is amusing that so many people know of the theft, but it's hardly convenient."

"I thought it might have been you that spread the word, Horm. You must be enjoying seeing Lisutaris heading for a fall."

"I am indeed. But it was not me that spread word throughout the city that she had lost the pendant."

Some melodious singing interrupts our conversation. Close to the shore, mermaids are forming a chorus.

"Are you responsible for this?" I ask.

Again Horm the Dead denies it.

"Of course I am not responsible. Why would I waste my time on such matters? Yesterday I was almost knocked over by a centaur. I presumed it was some sort of Turanian custom till some children started screaming in alarm. I suspect the magic space may be breaking through into the real world."

"I thought the same. Any idea how that might be happening?"

"None whatsoever. If it happens, it will certainly hasten your destruction."

"If it keeps spreading it might hasten yours."

The mermaids disappear. I'm not entirely certain where mermaids live, or if they really live anywhere. Unlike unicorns, centaurs, dryads and naiads, I've never actually met any.

Horm frowns.

"This should all have been simple. Sarin the Merciless receives the pendant and passes it to me. I leave the city bearing a mighty gift for Prince Amrag. I'm still not certain what went wrong. Glixius, possibly. He knows Sarin the Merciless. He may have learned of the affair earlier than I imagined."

"Possibly Sarin thought she might get more money from Glixius."

"Possibly. She is an efficient woman, but I have had occasion to criticise her for her venality."

"Who was Sarin meant to receive the pendant from?"

"That, I imagine, is the crux of your investigation," says Horm. "So I would not wish to spoil it for you by telling."

We've now walked back to the outskirts of the city, to the small gate in the walls, which is manned by a bored-looking guard.

"People are dying all over Turai, I believe," muses Horm. "Which is also puzzling. When I learned of the first deaths I presumed that they were connected to the pendant. It would certainly have that effect on the untrained mind. Yet the deaths are now so widespread that the jewel cannot be causing them all. It may be a sorcerous item but it can't be in more than one place at the same time."

"Yes, Horm, it's a mystery. And you saying you know nothing of the matter doesn't convince me."

Horm raises his eyebrows, just the slightest bit perturbed by me implying he may be lying.

"Tell me, Investigator, if you had by any chance stumbled across the jewel, what makes you think it would not have driven you mad?"

"Strong will power."

"You think so? I had not noticed. Sarin's description of you rolling around drunk in the gutter would not seem to fit a man of strong will power."

"Sarin is a liar."

Horm stares back down towards the sea. He points over to some rocks further along the coast.

"Another three bodies."

"Really?"

"From the Society of Friends, I believe. Probably followed Glixius and ended up killing each other.

"Glixius Dragon Killer," muses Horm. "Three times I have defeated him in combat, yet he seems undeterred. I suppose one should admire that, but really I find it tedious. Next time we meet I will certainly have to kill him."

"You're fond of promising to kill people, Horm."

Horm looks surprised. At the foot of the city walls a slight breeze makes his cloak wave in the air. I'm sweating in the heat but the half-Orc Sorcerer seems unaffected.

"Am I? Who else have I threatened to kill?"

"Me, for one."

"I hardly think that likely," says Horm. "Why would I threaten to kill you? There is not, and has never been, the slightest chance of you preventing me from carrying out my plans. You are beneath me, Thraxas, beneath me by a distance you cannot comprehend, Investigator who failed his sorcerous apprenticeship."

Horm smiles his malevolent smile

"Please give my regards to your fair companion Makri. If I am obliged to leave Turai without encountering her again, kindly inform her that when Prince Amrag sweeps this city away, I will try to save her."

Horm the Dead makes a formal bow and walks off along the foot of the city walls. I go through the gate and am immediately assaulted by the bustle of Twelve Seas.

An informative conversation. And polite. When Horm dismissed me as not worth bothering about he used only the most reasonable language. I'm thoughtful as I walk back towards the Avenging Axe. For all his superior power, Horm has no idea where the pendant is. And he can't find it by sorcery. Which gives me just as good a chance as him.

Better, in fact. I'm an Investigator. Number one chariot when you need something investigated. He's just a hugely powerful Sorcerer who happens to rule his own kingdom. And might have strange powers after coming back from the grave. I wonder again about the rumours of Horm having been dead.

I should have asked him about it. Difficult to work into the conversation, I suppose. I notice he mentioned Makri again. He was obviously quite taken by her. Probably it's been a long time since a woman punched him in the face. Might be the very sort of thing he's looking for in a relationship. I get the sudden unpleasant feeling that Horm's idea of an ideal woman might be one that he's brought back from the dead, in which case I can see Makri having some strong objections. Me too. Makri is aggravating as hell but I haven't quite reached the stage of wishing her dead.

Whether Horm is living, not living, or somewhere in-between, I'll find the pendant just to spite his arrogant face.

As I reach the hot, choking stretch of dirt that is Quintessence Street, I remember what Dandelion told me yesterday. She'd seen flashes of light over the beach. I wonder if she might have had anything else of interest to impart before I shut her up. I seek her out in the tavern and learn that she's upstairs in Makri's room.

I knock on the door, with no results, so I walk in and find Dandelion sitting on the floor, dangling a pendant in her hand. Hanging from the pendant is a green jewel, and the young woman is staring at it, transfixed.

"Give me that!" I yell.

She's lost in some other reality and shakes her head and blinks her eyes as I grab the pendant from her and cram it in my bag. I get ready to slug her in case she wakes up insane, not that it's going to be easy to tell.

"Pretty colours."

"Yes. Very pretty."

Dandelion smiles and lies down on the floor to sleep. She doesn't look like she's going to do anything violent. I'm puzzled. Everyone else who's looked through this jewel turned into a violent lunatic. Maybe you have to be that way inclined.

Perhaps the jewel doesn't make you mad if you're the sort of person who likes flowers and dolphins.

Leaving Dandelion to sleep it off, I take the pendant along to my room and wonder what to do with it. I have an almost overpowering urge to risk a glance, just to see what it's like. With some difficulty I overcome the urge and cram it in my desk drawer.

I've recovered the pendant. Smart work, though I say it myself. A huge stroke of luck, in reality, though I'm not going to admit that to anyone. Trust Dandelion to wander down to the polluted part of the beach and pick up the pendant from under the nose of Horm the Dead.

I wonder what to do now. The pendant can't stay here. It's too much of a risk. I'd best just get it back to Lisutaris as quickly as possible. I risk a quick trip downstairs to pick up a beer and I ask Gurd to look in on Dandelion to check she's okay.

"Trouble?"

"Probably not. She looked at something she shouldn't but I don't think it's done her any harm. Where's Makri?"

"Hunting for money."

"Huh?"

"She's getting another bet down with Moxalan."

Good point. With the three recent deaths I make the total thirty, and the case will end when I get the pendant back to Lisutaris. We ought to get some money on quickly. Suddenly life looks brighter. I can save Lisutaris, completing my case satisfactorily, and then make a healthy profit from Moxalan. Providing the city does not then disappear under a flood of unicorns and centaurs, it could be a good summer. I go back upstairs to look for Makri.

I find her in my room, standing next to my desk. She has the pendant in one hand, her black Orcish sword in the other, and a glazed look in her eyes.

"I am Makri, captain of armies," she says.

"Put the pendant down, Makri."

"Prepare to die," snarls Makri, and raises her sword.

Chapter Sixteen

About twenty years ago, I won the great swordfighting contest in far-off Samsarina. Every year this competition attracts the best fighters and gladiators from all over the world. I had to defeat a lot of good men. The savagery of the competition was legendary but I took on the best and beat them. Of course I was a lot younger then; a lot leaner, a lot hungrier. Even so, in the intervening years I've rarely met a person who could best me in close combat. But I'm thinking that Makri probably can. I've seen her fight too often to think otherwise.

Makri's under the influence of the jewel. It might slow her down. If so, I might defeat her, but a dead Makri doesn't seem like a great outcome either. I could try fleeing the room but Makri would probably have a knife in my back before I made it through the door. So I just raise my sword to defend myself, curse the heavens, and hope the effect of the jewel wears off quickly.

With my sword in my right hand and a knife in my left, I'm better armed than Makri. She's only carrying one sword, which is fortunate for me, as her own twin sword technique is something between a hurricane and a scything machine. Even so she quickly forces me back against the wall.

"Stop fighting, it's the jewel!" I scream, to no effect. Makri continues her relentless attack. From the blank look in her eyes and a certain unfamiliarity about her movements, I'm pretty sure she's fighting below her usual capacity, but even so I'm very hard pressed to hold her off. There's a fraction of a second where I see an opening, but I pull back from a lethal stroke and after that I'm pressed further and further back. Makri takes my blade on her own and with one smooth movement runs her sword down it. Such is the force of her black sword that the finger guard on my weapon is sliced off. Blood pours from my hand. I'm screaming at Makri to regain her senses but nothing is getting through. Damn this woman. I always knew she'd end up killing me somehow.

Desperation makes me forget my scruples and I fight with my full intensity, deciding that a dead Makri is better than a dead Thraxas, but she still forces me back till I've retreated the full length of the wall and am trapped against my desk. I'm about to make a desperate attempt at throwing my dagger into her unprotected torso when, with a movement I don't really see, Makri takes my dagger on the point of her sword and sends it spinning across the room. In another blinding movement she slashes downwards. I attempt to block the blow and my sword shatters into a thousand pieces.

She raises her weapon.

"It's time for your examination," I say.

Makri hesitates, confused.

"What?"

"Your examination. You have to get up and talk to the class. Right now. It's very important."

Makri's sword arm drops a few inches.

"I don't want to stand up in front of the class," she says. "It's scary."

"Well you have to do it. Right now."

Makri lowers her sword. She slouches across the room and sits down heavily on the couch.

"I won't do it," she says. "It's not fair."

I'm panting for breath. I feel like I'm about to die for lack of air. I've never been so hot. I pick up my water ewer and take a great draught. It's stale and warm. I offer some to Makri. She drinks it awkwardly.

"Did I pass the examination?" she asks.

Some of her natural expression has returned to her face. Abruptly she shakes her head and looks alert.

"What happened?"

I pick up the pendant from the floor.

"You looked into the jewel."

An expression of huge disappointment settles on her features.

"Am I not really captain of the armies?"

"I'm afraid not."

"Oh. I thought I was. It was good. We destroyed everything."

Makri drinks some more water and pours the last of it over her face.

"Did I pass the examination?"

"You haven't taken it yet. You've been confused from the jewel."

"I haven't taken it?"

Makri's shoulders droop. She looks almost comically glum.

"No examination pass. No captain of the armies. Of course. I'm just a waitress. What a lousy day."

By now I'm busy putting a little lotion on my cut fingers, a preparation made by Chiaraxi the local healer which is very good on wounds.

"Did I do that?" asks Makri.

"Yes. But I wasn't really fighting properly. I was just letting you burn yourself out. Naturally I didn't want to take advantage of your weakened state."

"I think I have an accurate memory of our combat," says Makri. All over the floor are the shards of my broken sword. I change the subject.

"Why were you looking in the drawer?"

"For money," says Makri.

"Of course. I should have known. Feel free to regard my money as your own."

"I was putting on a bet for both of us," says Makri, but she doesn't seem inclined to engage in our normal bickering. Instead she hauls herself to her feet, heavily, worn out from the effect of the jewel. Sweat has dampened her huge mane of hair and her pointed ears show through.

"Thanks for not killing me anyway," she says. Then she kisses me lightly on the cheek and slips out of the room.

"You're welcome," I say, to the door.

The pendant is dangling in my hand. It's a pretty thing, Elvish silverwork and a green gem of moderate size, well cut and sparkling in the few rays of sunlight that penetrate the drawn blinds of my office. This jewel is deadly. Anything other than a quick glance can suck you in. I'm tempted, but I don't succumb. I tear a scrap of cloth off an old tunic that serves as a towel, wrap it round the jewel then put it in my bag. It's time to take it to Lisutaris before it does any more harm.

As the rush of excitement brought on by combat fades, I find myself feeling well satisfied. You hire Thraxas to find a missing pendant and what happens? He finds your missing pendant. Whilst malevolent Sorcerers, evil killers, gangsters by the score and a whole army of government lackeys waste their energy in a fruitless search, I, Thraxas, have located the pendant without the help of sorcery or the assistance of a well-staffed intelligence service. Just solid, professional investigating and the willingness to do an honest day's work. There was something inevitable about it. It was more or less bound to happen. You have a problem? Call on Thraxas. This man delivers. In all of Turai, I doubt there's another person who could have retrieved the pendant.

There's a knock on my door. Avenaris, Lisutaris's secretary, walks into my office.

"Lisutaris has retrieved the pendant," she says.

I raise my eyebrows a fraction.

"Really?"

"Yes. This morning. She sent me to tell you to stop look-ing. And to pay you."

Avenaris lays some money on my desk. As always, behind her small, measured movements I can sense tension. She wants to get out of here as quickly as possible.

"How did Lisutaris locate the pendant?"

"She didn't tell me."

"Weren't you curious?"

"I should leave now. Be sure not to mention anything of this affair to anyone."

"Sure. We wouldn't want to raise any suspicions among the few people who don't know all about it already."

As ever, I'm curious about this nervous young woman whom Lisutaris is extremely keen to protect.

"You know anything about how the pendant went missing in the first place?" I demand.

"What?"

"You heard me. One minute you're looking after Lisutaris's bag, the next the pendant's gone missing. That always struck me as odd."

"I don't know why Lisutaris hired such a man as you," blurts Avenaris.

"Because I'm good at noticing things. I notice when people are more nervous than they should be. Why is Lisutaris so keen to protect you? Do you need protecting?"

"No."

"Lisutaris treat you well?"

"Lisutaris has always been very kind to me. I have to go now."

The tic on her face has started up again. I notice how skinny she is. Skinnier than Makri even. Not a young woman who enjoys her food. Not a woman who enjoys anything much, from the look of her. A memory floats into my mind. Young Barius, lying on the couch, gasping.

"Anyone ever call you Vee, Avenaris?" I say, abruptly.

The tic goes into overdrive. Avenaris puts her hand to her face to cover it. For a second I think she's going to faint.

"No!" she says. "Stop questioning me! Lisutaris told you not to."

With that she runs from my office. I'm still weighing up the implications of our encounter when Sarin breezes in, this time not pointing a crossbow at me.

"I'm disappointed," I say.

"At what?"

"I hoped you'd died when the warehouse collapsed."

"I didn't," says Sarin. She's not one for banter.

"What do you want?"

"I have a pendant to sell."

"A pendant?"

"Belonging to Lisutaris. I have recovered it. I had planned to sell it to Horm. Circumstances have now changed and I am prepared to sell it to either Lisutaris or the government, using you as an agent."

Lisutaris has the pendant. Now Sarin also has the pendant. Obviously they're both lying because I have the pendant. I spin Sarin along a little, trying to find out what she's up to.

"Circumstances have changed? Let me guess. Horm the Dead suspects you of double-crossing him and offering the pendant to Glixius Dragon Killer. Now you're worried you might find yourself on the wrong end of a heart attack spell."

No reaction from Sarin.

"What makes you think I'd act as your go-between?"

"You did before," says Sarin, which is true, though circumstances were different.

Sarin's price is five thousand gurans.

"Worth it to Lisutaris, to save her skin."

"Maybe, Sarin. But one day you're going to come to grief, meddling with the affairs of Sorcerers. They're not all going to fall for you like Tas of the Eastern Lightning. What did you do to him? A simple stab in the back?"

"Something like that," replies Sarin the Merciless. "Lisutaris has till tomorrow to come up with the money. Which she'd better do. My next approach will be to the Palace itself. They'll pay well to keep the pendant from the Orcs."

"It doesn't worry you, selling state secrets to the enemy?"

"Not at all."

"If the Orcs invade the west, I doubt they'll spare you."

Sarin looks at me quite blankly, and I get the sudden odd impression that she'd welcome death. Unwilling to engage in further conversation, she slips quietly from my office, leaving me to mull over her offer. I find myself admiring her nerve. She doesn't even have the pendant, yet here she is, still trying to profit from the affair.

I need beer. I head downstairs to get myself around a Happy Guildsman jumbo-sized tankard. Gurd is still as miserable as a Niojan whore, and Makri is resting upstairs, leaving the incompetent Dandelion to struggle with the task of pulling the ale. By the time she finally plants my Happy Guildsman in front of me, I could have walked to the next tavern and downed a few.

"You're looking thoughtful," says Dandelion, who, I think, has learned from Gurd that the clientele often enjoy a word with the bartender.

"Too many pendants."

"What?"

I shake my head. If I ever reach the stage of discussing my work with Dandelion, it'll be time to retire.

"What did you see when you looked in the jewel?"

"Lots of nice colours. And some flowers."

It didn't do her any harm. Everyone else it drove mad. Dandelion just saw some pretty colours. Maybe there's something to be said for walking around in bare feet. I warn her not to relate her experience to anyone, and tell her I'd like another tankard as soon as she's finished struggling with the large order from three sailmakers who are shouting for drinks from the far end of the counter. They've just completed the re-sailing of a trireme and they have a lot of money to spend. More sailmakers arrive and start demanding ale and bragging about the work they've done and the money they've earned. It's not a bad life being a sailmaker if the city's merchant trade is healthy, which it is. Plenty of ships, plenty of work.

I secure another beer and leave them to it. I'm unsure of what to do now. Visit Lisutaris, I suppose. She claims to have the pendant. But she can't have it. I've got it. And why send me the message? I can understand why she might be faking something for the benefit of the Consul, but there's no point lying to me.

Casax, the local Brotherhood boss, appears before I have time to sit down. It's surprising how busy my office can be at times. You'd think I'd earn more.

"You want to buy this pendant everyone's been looking for?" he asks.

"Why do you want to know?"

"Because I have it," says Casax. "One of my men found it in Kushni. But I'm a patriotic guy. I'm not going to let it fall into the hands of one of these outsiders. I'll let it go back where it belongs, so long as there's a profit in it for me."

"I know nothing of any missing pendant."

"I know you know nothing of any missing pendant. But if you did know anything about a missing pendant, a pendant which contains a jewel which will give our top Sorcerer some advance warning about when the Orcs might attack, would you want to buy it back?"

"When you put it like that, maybe. What's your price?"

"Three thousand gurans. In gold."

"That's a lot of gold for a patriotic guy."

"I have to make a living."

I ask to see the pendant.

"It's in a safe place," says Casax.

He expects me to trust him. Which I probably would, normally, in a matter like this. The Brotherhood boss would not waste his time trying to sell me an item he didn't have. So why is he trying to do it now? I can't figure it out. The pendant is in my bag. I know it is. I checked just a moment ago. Are these people all trying to work some scam, or is this some effect of the sorcerous madness that's been breaking out all over? Maybe Casax really thinks he does have the pendant. Maybe he thinks he can talk to the unicorns.

"There was a centaur in my tavern last night," he says, which makes me think that my guess might not be so far off.

"Really?"

"Yeah. I never seen one before. You think it would be strange, being half man and half horse, but the centaur didn't seem to mind."

"What happened to it?"

"It drank some beer then disappeared. Is all this stuff going to end now the pendant's been found? It's bad for business, strange things happening all over the city. Makes my men forget what they should be doing. I sent two guys out last night to pick up a debt and they came back spouting some stuff about mermaids in fountains. I'd have killed them on the spot if the centaur hadn't showed up, which did give their story some credibility. Bad for business, though."

I admit to Casax that I don't know if the strangeness will end. I don't know if it's really connected to the pendant.

"The Sorcerers Guild should sort it out. Normal people shouldn't be coping with this sort of thing."

I tell Casax I'll put his offer to Lisutaris. I wonder what Lisutaris will say when I do. I don't know why they're all lying. I can't think straight. At least I know why I can't think straight. It's because I haven't had a decent pie or portion of venison stew for days. Since Tanrose left, I haven't eaten one thing that truly satisfied me. A man can't be expected to do his best work in these circumstances. I decide to visit Tanrose. Possibly I might be able to persuade her to come back to the Avenging Axe. Failing that, she might offer me dinner.

I disturb Makri's rest.

"I have to go out. Stake some money on forty. It's still going up."

"Okay."

"I'm going to see Tanrose. You want I should bring you back a pie?"

Makri shakes her head. She has little enthusiasm for food.

Chapter Seventeen

Tanrose is living with her mother on the top floor of a dark stone tenement between Twelve Seas and Pashish. Five flights up, with a stairway that could use some cleaning and a few more torches to light the way. As I arrive, Tanrose is laying dinner out on the table, one of the few strokes of good fortune I've had all summer. Not wishing to be impolite, I accept her offer of a meal. Once at the table, I lose all self-control and take second, third and fourth helpings of everything. Tanrose is amused, as is her mother, an elderly woman with white hair who already knows my appetite by reputation.

"I like to see a man eat well," she says, and brings me another pie from the larder, I hesitate. With Tanrose no longer bringing in her wages from the Avenging Axe, there might not be much money to go around. There again, I don't want to appear impolite. I eat the pie.

"Tanrose, you have to come back to the Avenging Axe. The population of Twelve Seas is starving to death. There's misery everywhere, particularly in my rooms."

Tanrose asks if Gurd sent me.

"No."

"So he's too useless even to send a message," says Tanrose, which is true, I suppose. I try to excuse him.

"He spent his life fighting. There was no finer companion for killing Niojans. It's not easy for a warrior to settle down. I know he loves you. He just doesn't want to say it."

"He doesn't have any trouble in saying he doesn't like my bookkeeping."

I contrive to look hopeless. A few minutes of this sort of conversation is all I can ever manage. I've no idea how to bring together sundered couples. I don't remember ever caring about a sundered couple before.

"What will it take to bring you back? An apology? A marriage proposal? Or would a bunch of flowers do it?"

"It would help."

"I'm always surprised how much you like flowers, Tanrose." Tanrose smiles.

"It's the thought behind them."

"Is it such a great thought?"

"It worked with Makri, didn't it?"

On several previous occasions when Makri had taken offence at some of my wilder outbursts of invective—criticism of her morals or her ears or her clothes, or maybe a few other things—I had managed to calm the troubled waters with flowers, not something I would ever have thought of myself unless prompted by Tanrose. Naturally this entire process was greatly humiliating to a man such as myself, involving much mirth from the flower sellers, Gurd, and the assembled drunks at the Avenging Axe, but it seemed preferable to the terrible atmosphere caused by Makri storming round in a bad mood for weeks on end, which she's quite capable of.

"It did work. But only because Makri was too naive to realise I was faking it."

"Faking it?"

"Sure. I don't care if the woman is upset or not. It just makes it difficult getting a quiet beer. Have you noticed how much more annoying she's got recently?"

"No, I don't think so."

"There's definitely something different," I say.

"Maybe the difference is with you," suggests Tanrose.

I look at her suspiciously.

"What do you mean by that?"

"Ever since last year when Makri had her first romantic encounter with that Elf on Avula you've been in a bad mood. And I notice you're really giving her a hard time as well."

"So?"

"So I'm beginning to think the gossips might be right."

I'm not liking the way this conversation is going.

"Right about what?" I demand.

"Maybe you wouldn't mind ending up with a young companion to keep you warm in winter."

I practically choke on my pie.

"Tanrose! Have you lost your mind?"

I rise to my feet.

"I came here to try and smooth things out between you and Gurd, and now you're making crazy insinuations. Of course I give Makri a hard time. She's an insane half-Orc menace to society who'll probably get me killed one of these days. Kindly never insinuate anything again."

Tanrose is laughing.

"I apologise, Thraxas. Sit down and finish your pie. You know I can't just arrive back in the Avenging Axe. Might as well send Gurd a message saying he's welcome to walk all over me. He has to make the first move."

"What if Gurd thinks *you* have to make the first move?"

There doesn't seem any ready answer to this. It's the sort of insoluble problem that led to my marriage falling apart a long time ago. I'm grateful for the food, but even a brief conversation about Tanrose and Gurd's relationship has made me feel very uneasy. I leave after expressing my own profoundest wishes that Tanrose hurry back to the Avenging Axe where she belongs.

Right outside the tenement, some magical silver doves are fluttering around gaily. I bat them out of the way, not being in the mood for magical silver doves. Further down the street I come across a detachment of Civil Guards and at the next corner a squadron of the King's troops. The city is becoming nervous. Alarm is spreading at the widespread reports of mysterious apparitions and unexplained deaths. Personally I'm more alarmed at Tanrose making a joke about me desiring Makri to keep me warm on a winter's night. It was in very poor taste. I hurry into a tavern to wash away the bad taste with copious amounts of beer.

Inside the tavern I pick up a copy of the *Renowned and Truthful Chronicle*, freshly printed. One side of the single sheet is entirely taken up with reports of sightings of magical creatures, golden trees and such like, and the other details the surprising number of deaths there have been in the city in the past few days. Even by Turai's standards, the population is decreasing at an alarming rate.

Who is responsible for this? thunders the *Chronicle. And why has no attempt been made to arrest the renegade Tribune Thraxas?*

What? I shake my head, barely able to believe what I'm reading. I find myself shrinking in my seat, hoping no one recognises me as I hurriedly scan the rest of the article.

All signs indicate that Thraxas—a so called Investigator in Twelve Seas of whom we have had reason to complain before—is heavily involved in the affair. Our enquiries show that in the space of three days this man has been at the scene of a great many unexplained deaths. Several landlords, for instance, report that Thraxas—a huge man of bestial appetites—visited their taverns only minutes before a series of savage murders were committed, leaving swiftly after searching the bodies for valuables.

Furthermore, Thraxas, a known associate of several renegade Sorcerers, has been repeatedly questioned by the Consul and his deputy after an attempt was made to blackmail Lisutaris, Mistress of the Sky. While we have no absolute proof that Thraxas was behind this attempt, he has reportedly been trying to sell various personal items belonging to the Sorcerer, including a diary and some items of jewellery. Reports from other sources indicate that guards at the Guild College were forced to eject him after he menaced Professor Toarius over a sum of five gurans.

Although it cannot yet be proved that Thraxas is responsible for the mysterious apparitions that have been troubling the city, he is known to have dabbled in the sorcerous arts, and may be in possession of several devastating Orcish spells (he is fluent in the Orcish language, and is rumoured to have various Orcish associates). It has recently come to light that he once threw down his shield and fled the field of battle, an offence for which he will shortly face charges in court. Why is this man still at liberty? And why, we would like to know, was he ever granted the office of Tribune? Even in a city as corrupt as Turai, surely a man of such reputation should not be able to bribe his way into lucrative government positions . . .

It goes on for a while in a similar manner. I'm devastated. I've been denounced by the *Chronicle* before, but never so damagingly. Reading the remarks about throwing down my shield, I feel a rage swelling up inside me the like of which I can rarely remember, and I wonder why the hell I haven't killed Vadinex yet. Kill him, then pay a visit to the *Chronicle* and beat the editor. Damn these people, no one says things like that about me and gets away with it. I throw back my beer and storm out of the tavern, intent on doing some violence to someone, and quickly.

I'm intercepted by Makri in Quintessence Street.

"Thraxas, I've been looking for you."

"Did you see the article?"

"Everyone saw it. You can't come back to the Avenging Axe. The Civil Guards are waiting to arrest you. They have a warrant."

"The Guards? Damn them. Every time the *Chronicle* criticises them they think they have to do something about it. When I get hold of that editor I'm going to—"

"What about the pendant?" asks Makri.

"I've still got it."

"Then why did three men die in the next street just an hour ago for no good reason? I thought the strange deaths were all related to the pendant, but it's been with you. They can't have looked at it."

I admit I'm baffled.

"I thought it was all pendant-related too. Maybe it's some madness unleashed by Horm the Dead. Anyway, I have to get the pendant back to Lisutaris. Once that's done, she can get back to looking after the sorcerous requirements of the city. She can sort out the unicorns and all the rest."

"How are you going to get it back to Lisutaris? It's not safe for you to travel around the city."

Four Civil Guards are heading in our direction. I withdraw into the cover of a shop doorway as they pass. In the dim evening light they don't pay much attention to me.

"I'll just have to make my way there by the back streets."

Makri points out that it's not going to be easy for me to even approach Lisutaris's house.

"They're bound to be watching. Everyone knows there's something going on with Lisutaris. If you turn up at her door, they'll just haul you away."

"You're right."

I try to think.

"Do you have any idea what sort of costume I should wear?" asks Makri.

"What?"

"For the masked ball tomorrow. Lisutaris says I have to go in a costume. I'm not familiar with this concept. I was going to look it up in the Imperial Library but I didn't have time, what with everything that's being going on."

"This is no time to be discussing costumes."

"But I don't know what to wear," says Makri, sounding unhappy. "I don't want everyone to laugh at me."

It's really too much. A man can only stand so much harassment in his own city. I firmly resolve to slip out of the city under cover of darkness and never come back.

"All the rich people will have really fancy costumes, I expect," continues Makri. "How am I meant to compete with that?"

"Wear your armour," I suggest.

"My armour?"

Makri brought a fine suit of light body armour with her

from the Orc gladiator pit. Made of chainmail and black leather, it's an arresting sight, and the Orcish metalwork is not something you see in Turai every day.

"Why not? You're meant to be going there as Lisutaris's bodyguard, so it would be appropriate."

"But am I meant to be appropriate?" says Makri. "Don't Senators go dressed as pirates and things like that?"

"I believe so."

"So if I'm really there as a bodyguard, shouldn't I be dressed as maybe a philosopher?"

Night is closing in. I should probably flee the city soon. I explain to Makri that while it is customary for people to attend these masked ball in costumes which may bear no relation to their normal station in life, it's not something that is governed by rules.

"I doubt if Cicerius is going to dress up as a pirate. Probably he'll go as the Deputy Consul, but wear some discreet little mask. Only the more extrovert sort of Senator will turn up in outlandish garb."

Makri nods her head.

"I see. So really, any costume is fine?"

"I expect so."

"I suppose a person might gain some social status by turning up in an especially fine costume. It would get noticed, I imagine."

"Yes, Makri, you seem to be getting the hang of it. Could we stop discussing it now? I seem to have some other pressing matters to attend to."

"Okay," says Makri. "I just wanted to get it clear. From what you say, my bodyguard costume should do fine. And after all, how many people will be there in a full set of light Orcish armour? Not many, I'm sure. And I don't often get the chance to wear the helmet. Thanks, Thraxas."

Makri now looks happy. Obviously the costume problem was preying on her mind. Despite my numerous problems, I still manage to get annoyed that I'm not invited. Until it strikes me that the masked ball does present an excellent opportunity for getting myself unnoticed into Lisutaris's house.

"Of course," I exclaim. "I'll dress up as something and just waltz in tomorrow evening. I give the pendant back to Lisutaris, she shows it to the Consul and the main problem disappears. Once the threat to national security is out of the way, I can start proving I haven't been going round killing or blackmailing people. Lisutaris will speak up for me once I've solved her problem."

Makri purses her lips.

"But you're not invited."

"So what? I'll forge an invitation."

"You just can't stand it that I'm going to the ball and you're not invited," says Makri.

"That has nothing to do with it."

"Very likely. Admit it, Thraxas, you've been plotting to go to Lisutaris's ball from the moment you learned I was going. It's really not mature behaviour."

"Will you stop this? I don't give a damn that you're going to some party. I have no wish to attend and am merely planning to do so in order to bring the case to a conclusion."

"You don't fool me for a moment," says Makri, and looks cross. "What if you're found out? People will think I let you in."

"Who's going to think that?"

"Everyone."

"Well so what? Since when did you care what Turai's aristocracy thought of you?"

"I just don't want to be humiliated at my first major social function."

I clutch my hand to my brow, something I don't do that often.

"I can't believe we're having this conversation. Are you still dazed from staring into the jewel? I have important business to take care of."

Makri remains convinced that I wish merely to attend the ball.

"You had better not embarrass me."

"Me embarrass you? Who was it got so wasted at the Sorcerers Assemblage that I had to pick her up and carry her out of the hall? Who threw up in front of the Deputy Consul?"

"That was different. The Sorcerers Assemblage was full of people getting drunk and throwing up. Almost every Sorcerer, from what I remember."

In the next street a huge mushroom of flame suddenly spurts from the rooftops. Whistles sound and Guards appear from every direction. I shrink further back in the doorway. The flames turn green then disappear.

"Another apparition. They're getting worse."

"More unicorns in Twelve Seas today," agrees Makri.

"I have to get going now. I'm going to hide down by the docks. I have the pendant safe with me. Providing Horm or Glixius don't find me, I'll meet you at Lisutaris's house tomorrow. See what you can find out about the secretary."

"What?"

"Avenaris. I have strong suspicions about her. I think she had some involvement with Barius."

"Why?"

"Investigator's intuition. One other thing. The body count is way out of control. People are dying everywhere. I don't exactly know how Moxalan is going to prove which deaths are connected to me, but in case it turns out they all are, get the last of the money and put a bet on sixty."

"Sixty?"

"That's right. See you tomorrow."

"What are you going to do for a costume?"

"Good question. You'll have to find something for me."

"Just fit on a pair of tusks and go as an elephant," suggests Makri, who's still showing signs of resentment at my plan to attend the ball. I ignore her jibe.

"Bring me my toga."

"You have a toga?"

"Yes, from my days at the Palace. It's under the bed. And some sort of mask. You can find one in the market."

"It won't be as good as my bodyguard costume," says Makri. "Where will I find you?"

"I'm going to hide in the stock pens at the harbour. There's a warehouse there waiting for some horses to be shipped in, it'll be empty for a day or two."

Makri agrees to bring me my toga there tomorrow. I steal away along Quintessence Street, heading off down the first alley I come to. With my excellent knowledge of Twelve Sea's back roads and alleyways, I should be able to make my way to the harbour undetected by the Civil Guards. It's lucky I went to see Tanrose. Without her food inside me, I'd never make it through the night.

Chapter Eighteen

I spend a not too uncomfortable night on a pile of hay in a warehouse and remain there as the sun climbs into the sky. The warehouse has various stalls and troughs and is used as a pen for animals brought into the city by sea. Fortunately the owner is still waiting for his imported horses to arrive, so I have the place to myself. Apart from the strong smell of livestock, it doesn't compare too badly with the Avenging Axe for comfort. I find some bread and dried meat in an unattended office which keeps me going. A watchman looks in every few hours, which has me diving under the hay, but other than that I'm undisturbed. I'm reasonably certain that the Civil Guards won't look for me here, but I'm half expecting Horm or Glixius to track me down. No one arrives, however, and I spend the day lounging in the hay, eating dried meat, and mulling things over.

It's the first quiet day I've had for a long time. After nine or ten hours lounging in the hay my head is clearer and I'm feeling rested. Maybe it's not so bad being a horse. In the early evening Makri wanders into the warehouse, whistling softly. I emerge from the hay to greet her.

"Did you bring my toga?"

"Toga, sandals and a mask. And beer."

Makri empties the contents of her bag. I'm immensely grateful for the beer. I drink it while I get the toga out. It could be cleaner but it'll do.

"They're difficult to wear, you know. You have to drape it just right. Any sudden movement and it's liable to fall off. That's why you never see Senators running around, it's too risky. What sort of mask did you bring?"

Makri has purchased a cheap mask from the market. It's a comic representation of Deputy Consul Cicerius.

"It was the only one they had."

Makri wonders why I don't give her the pendant to return. I point out that it's already driven her mad once.

"You'd be tempted to look again."

"You're right," says Makri. "It was so good being captain of the armies."

"What have you done to your hair?" I ask, suddenly noticing that her already voluminous mane is looking even fuller than usual.

"I washed it in a lotion of pixlas herbs."

"What?"

"They sell it at the market. It adds volume. And conditioning. Hey, I'm not turning up at Lisutaris's ball looking like a tramp. It will be full of Senators' wives. I have to go now."

"To do your make-up?"

"Possibly."

Around the time of the Sorcerers Assemblage, Makri encountered Copro, one of the city's finest beauticians. She was later forced to kill him after he turned out to be a rather deadly enemy, but even so, it had an effect. Previously dismissive of upper-class frippery, Makri can now be found painting her nails.

"How are things out there?"

"Hell," replies Makri. "Unicorns, centaurs, fire, death, delusions. The city's in chaos. I really wish I could afford to go to the beautician. Lisutaris has a team of them booked for the entire day. Maybe if I turn up early she'll let me share."

Makri departs. Night is approaching and I struggle into my toga and put the mask in my bag. I try my best to hide my hair down the back of my toga. Then, hoping that I look something like a Senator who's on his way to a masked ball, I emerge on to the streets of Twelve Seas to be immediately ridiculed by some small children who wonder out loud if I'm a sorcerous apparition. I chase them off with some language they're not expecting to hear from a Senator.

"That's no way to talk to children."

Captain Rallee is looking at me with some amusement. Behind him are three Civil Guards.

"You're under arrest, Senator Thraxas."

I'm carrying one spell. I mutter the correct arcane words and the Captain and his companions fall to the ground. The sleep spell is very effective, one of the few I can still use with authority. Unfortunately I've now run out of magic completely and won't be able to load any more into my memory till I consult my grimoire. I had been hoping to save that one spell for the masked ball in case I run into trouble there.

Of course, having used a spell on a Guards captain I'm already in big trouble. Resisting arrest by use of sorcery is a very serious crime. I hurry off and wave down the first landus I see.

"The home of Lisutaris, Mistress of the Sky. At great speed."

I squirm around a little, trying not to sit on my sword, which is concealed under my toga. Only a few months ago I saw a group of travelling actors performing a sketch at the Pleasure Gardens in which a bumbling Senator's toga fell off just as the princess walked into the room. I wouldn't bet against that happening tonight. I wonder if Lisutaris has invited any princesses. Quite probably. The young Princess Du-Akai is a keen socialite. Also a former client of mine, in a confidential matter. I'd best try to keep out of her way.

I keep my head down all the way through town. When we join the throng of vehicles making their way into Truth is Beauty Lane, I risk a glance. All around me are splendid carriages filled with people in elaborate costumes. Sitting in a hired landus with an old toga and an unimpressive mask, I already feel cheap. I still figure I can carry it off. I won't be the only one in attendance without two gurans to rub together. You don't have to look too far among Turai's upper classes to find men so far in debt they're never coming out.

I toss some money at the driver, leap out of the landus and lose myself in a crowd of giggling young ladies who're swaying up the driveway dressed as dancers. Unless they really are dancers. Assuming the air of a benevolent patriarch shepherding his flock, I stride confidently through the doors, take a glass of wine from a servant and look for the party.

Mostly the party is outside, and I'm directed by a series of servants through to the extensive grounds in the back where music is coming from every corner and a great throng of people, all elegantly costumed and masked, are walking in and out of a series of large marquees. It strikes me for the first time that it may not be easy to immediately locate Lisutaris. I'd hoped she might be welcoming guests at the door, but she's obviously in the midst of the throng, unless she's still getting dressed. Having worked for the woman last year, I've had experience of the staggering amount of time she can take to get ready. Still, I'm guessing that as a matter of pride Lisutaris will be wearing the fanciest costume on view, so I look around for anyone who looks particularly fabulous. Unfortunately there are a lot to choose from. The gardens contain all manner of masked guests, from men who, like myself, are merely clad in their formal togas with the addition of a mask, to others who've spent weeks preparing the most elaborate of outfits. Pirates, soldiers, Elves, famous historical figures, snow pixies, angels, Barbarians, all manner of masks and costumes. I approach a fantastic-looking figure clad in a rather graceful eagle's mask, hoping that it might be Lisutaris, but am disappointed to hear the figure complaining bitterly to her companion about the price of merchandise in the market these days. Lisutaris would regard it as beneath her to complain of such a thing.

I wonder where Makri is. She might be upstairs sharing a beautician with Lisutaris. More to the point, sharing a thazis pipe, which means they might not appear for hours. I'm becoming uncomfortable carrying the pendant around. I keep fearing that the latent power it contains might leak out somehow and affect me. Already I've seen a wood nymph that seemed alarmingly real. I should return the pendant as swiftly as possible. There's no telling when Consul Kalius will take it into his head to confront Lisutaris and demand to see it. And if Horm the Dead really does plan to pay us a visit, I'd rather the jewel was with Lisutaris than me. Let her deal with his sorcerous malevolence. I must waste no time in hunting for Lisutaris.

I need beer. The only unmasked people in the gardens are the waiters.

"I don't suppose there's any beer on offer?" I ask one of them, eyeing his tray of wine with dissatisfaction.

"I believe they have beer in the blue marquee, for the musicians," he informs me.

Still not wasting any time in hunting for Lisutaris, I make a swift detour to the blue marquee, where couples dance to the stately music played by a small orchestra. It's a good steer by the waiter. No professional musicians are going to play the whole night fuelled only by vintage wine. Beer is available and I avail myself of it, raising a tankard to the band in appreciation. I watch the dancers while I wait for more beer. They're performing the slow, formal and rather intricate court dances as taught by Turai's dancing masters and performed in the best houses. I did actually learn something of the sort while working at the Palace, though it wasn't an art I was ever comfortable with. A man dressed as some sort of jester guides a woman in a nun's costume round, leading off the next part of the dance, and a great troop of pirates and Barbarians follow them round the floor. From the number of dancers in the marquee and the amount of civilised revellers outside, I'd say that Lisutaris's masked ball was a success. I should find her. The night being exceedingly warm, I take in some more beer, just to be on the safe side, then set off, intending to try the house. Outside the marquee I meet the waiter again.

"Have you seen Lisutaris?" I ask. "Do you know what costume she's wearing?"

He looks down his nose at me.

"Please!" he exclaims. "Are you unaware of the etiquette of the masked ball?"

"Which piece of etiquette would that be?"

"One must never enquire who anyone is," he says, haughtily. "It's the height of bad manners."

I head for the house, rather abashed. Coming towards me is the Deputy Consul. Cicerius, though masked, is wearing his official toga, easily recognisable. If he catches me here wearing my cheap Cicerius mask, trouble will follow. I leap into the bushes to hide. There I find myself face to face with a large man incongruously garbed as a snow pixie.

"I'm the richest man in the world," he says.

"Well good for you."

His knees sag and he tumbles to the ground. I kneel over him. He's dead. Another victim of the jewel? He can't be. The jewel is safe in my bag. I take off the man's mask but it's no one I recognise. Just a Senator who always dreamed of being the richest man in the world. I feel something hard beneath my knee. It's a familiar-looking pendant. The missing pendant, in fact. I open the small bag I've strapped under my toga. It also contains the missing pendant. I now have two missing pendants. There's only meant to be one. Everyone was clear on that. I scoop the new pendant into my bag and make for the house. As I'm nearing the back door, a unicorn trots across my path. People applaud, thinking it to be part of the entertainment.

Indoors the staff are directing guests through the hallways into the gardens, not allowing anyone to climb the stairs to the Sorcerer's private apartments. I wait for a quiet moment before slipping a few gurans to a boy in a smart red tunic.

"Private business," I say. "Look the other way."

He looks the other way and I hurry up the staircase. I'm familiar with this house and know that if Lisutaris has not yet made her entrance she'll be in the suite of rooms at the far end, doing her hair, or smoking thazis. Makri appears in the corridor, striding along confidently in her dark Orcish armour.

"Makri—"

She walks past, completely ignoring me.

"To hell with you," I call after her. She must still be upset that I've gatecrashed the ball. I find Lisutaris's main salon and dive through the door.

"Lisutaris, we have big problems."

Lisutaris is sitting in front of a mirror, with a stylist beside her doing her hair. Consul Kalius is sitting nearby on a couch. He's dressed as a pirate but has discarded his mask. Makri is standing by the window.

The Consul rises.

"What problems?"

"The musicians are running out of beer."

The Consul laughs, and compliments me on my amusing Cicerius mask. Makri—who can't be here because she just walked down the corridor—looks surprised to see me. Lisutaris is annoyed.

"Who are you?" she demands.

I can't identify myself in front of Kalius before I've cleared things up.

"Etiquette prevents me from saying," I reply.

"Well get the hell out of my rooms before I have my staff toss you out into the street," says Lisutaris.

She's wearing a magnificent winged costume, the Angel of the Southern Hurricane, I believe.

"The musicians really need beer. And Deputy Consul Cicerius is looking for the Consul on a matter of great urgency."

Lisutaris now recognises my voice and looks alarmed. She turns to the Consul.

"Perhaps you should—"

Kalius smiles. He's looking quite jovial. Not like a man who's just denounced the head of the Sorcerers Guild for betraying the city.

"I will sort things out," he says, affably. "You mustn't be disturbed while you're making ready for your grand entrance. The musicians need beer, you say? I'm sure I can rectify that. And Cicerius wishes to see me? No doubt on some affair of state. The Deputy Consul can never bring himself to fully relax on these occasions."

He rises, bows formally to Lisutaris and departs. I take off my mask.

"The Consul's looking happy."

"What are you doing here?" demands Lisutaris.

"He couldn't stand not being invited," says Makri. "It's completely childish. Just like the Elvish princess in the story."

"What story?"

"'The Elvish Princess Who Was Completely Childish.'"

Not for the first time I glare at Makri with loathing.

"There is no such story."

"Yes there is. I translated it last year."

"Is this true?" demands Lisutaris. "You have invaded my house in a fit of pique?"

"A fit of pique!" I roar. "Have you forgotten you hired me to do a job? To retrieve the fantastically important jewel? Well I've done it."

"But I've already done that," protests Lisutaris. "I retrieved the jewel myself. I have just been showing it to the Consul. Didn't you notice how cheerful he was?"

"Well this might make everybody less cheerful," I say, and produce the two pendants from my bag.

"Obvious fakes," says Lisutaris.

"Oh yes? There's a dead man in the bushes who doesn't agree. Take a look."

Lisutaris takes one of the pendants and stares deeply into it. She frowns. She studies the other jewel. She places it on her bureau and opens a drawer, producing a third jewel.

"They are all real."

"You didn't mention there were three of them," I say.

"There aren't three of them! There's only one. But these are all the real one."

"Well that's a mystery," I say, sitting down on the couch. "But it does explain why people have been being trampled by unicorns all over Turai even when I recovered the jewel. The place is awash with sorcerous pendants."

"You say there is a dead man in my garden?"

"Yes. But well hidden in the bushes. We might expect worse. Apparitions are still going on, and I know of several other people who claim to have the pendant. Which they might have. God knows how many of these things there are out there, each of them potentially lethal. If they all turn up in the same place I'm guessing we're in for a memorable party."

There's a discreet knock on the door and a maid enters.

"Centaurs are destroying the green marquee, miss," she says, politely.

Lisutaris looks to Makri.

"I'll deal with it," says Makri, and puts on her helmet before hurrying off.

"You feel the need to stay?" says Lisutaris.

"There are some things we should discuss. Like how there are suddenly a lot of pendants. And what we're going to do about it."

"I really cannot be dealing with this sort of thing at my ball," protests the Sorcerer. "It's time for my entrance."

"Don't you realise what's about to happen out there? If centaurs are eating your marquee it means they're being produced by more of these jewels. Anyone in the gardens is quite likely to die because they find one and stare into it. Or else there will be a panic when a marquee appears to catch fire. Or maybe really catches fire. And don't forget Horm the Dead has promised to pay you a visit. Which might mean another appearance from Glixius Dragon Killer. Also, Sarin the Merciless is still trying to sell a pendant. I'd say this ball might be remembered as the social occasion when everybody died."

"You really know how to spoil a party, don't you?" says Lisutaris, angrily, like it's all my fault.

"Do you have any idea how the pendant might have mysteriously multiplied itself? Is there a spell which could do that?"

Lisutaris is still fussing with her hair in the mirror. It's the largest, most perfectly made dressing mirror I've ever seen. Buying a piece of glass like that must have been prohibitively expensive. I doubt if there's a better one at the Imperial Palace.

"It might possibly be done by a very experienced practitioner," mutters Lisutaris. "Though it would take an immense amount of skill. But who would do such a thing?"

I shrug.

"Look at the people who've been involved. Horm, Glixius. There's no telling what their motives might be. Horm has been keen to discredit you from the start. Maybe he thought he could take the pendant back for Prince Amrag and still make you look foolish by leaving some counterfeits behind. Maybe he cunningly planned it so they'd all end up here and destroy your guests. Good way to get rid of Turai's leaders. Whoever's behind it we have to do something. You ought to know better than me that having this many sorcerous items together is highly dangerous. What if the copies are unstable? Either the magic space is going to invade your gardens or there's going to be an almighty explosion."

Last century, for reasons which were never clear, the great Simnian Sorcerer Balanius the Most Powerful made a duplicate of himself. By all accounts it was a perfect copy, but when he shook hands with himself there was an explosion which flattened his city. You can still see the crater in Simnia.

Lisutaris drags herself away from the mirror.

"We don't know that there are any more in the vicinity. There might be only these three. I can contain them."

"I feel that there are others."

"How?"

"Intuition."

Lisutaris is dubious about my intuition. She crosses to the window and gazes out at the gardens for a moment or two.

"You're right, unfortunately. I can sense more of the pendants. I'm not sure how many. You may also be correct about their instability. Copying a sorcerous item of such power is almost impossible to get right."

Lisutaris walks over to a painting on her wall. She speaks to it and the painting shifts to one side. Behind the painting there's a safe. She mutters a rather long series of ancient words and it opens. From the safe she withdraws a bag.

"This is made of red Elvish cloth. If you put the pendants in here it should dampen the effect. But be careful not to let anyone see what you're doing. It's illegal for any private citizen, even me, to own this cloth. The King will be down on me like a bad spell if he knows I have it."

I notice that Lisutaris seems to be talking about me doing the dirty work.

"You want me to gather up an unknown number of dangerous sorcerous pendants? I've been nervous enough carrying round one. Can't you help?"

"I have a ball to host. What will people say if I'm scurrying round with a bag rather than mingling with my guests? And is this not what I hired you for? To protect my reputation? Do not let Consul Kalius discover what you're doing. I've just managed to convince him I didn't lose the original.

Having fake gems turn up isn't going to make me look good. Take this."

Lisutaris hands me a copper bracelet.

"This will glow when in the vicinity of any sorcerous item."

"It's glowing right now."

"That's because my rooms are full of sorcerous items. It will help you to search in the gardens. I hope Makri managed to disperse the centaurs before they did much damage. If you find any more bodies, have my staff remove them discreetly."

"I really don't like this."

"We have no choice. I will do my best to control any appuritions. I have to go. I'm due to lead off a dance with Prince Frisen Akan."

"Take care he doesn't tread on your toes."

"I expect he will."

I step out into the corridor. I'm heading for the gardens but I hesitate. Avenaris's private rooms are on the next floor. With no one around to observe me, I hurry upstairs to check them out. Lisutaris will fume if she catches me, but what is she going to do? She needs me to do her dirty work outside. I remember I forgot to ask about the other person in Orcish armour who I thought was Makri. Maybe it's nothing. No, it's something bad, I know it. Might it be Sarin? I'll deal with it later.

Avenaris's room is locked. I try a minor word of power, to no effect. I put my weight against the door and push. It gives slowly. It takes a good door to resist my bulk. Inside I find a suite of rooms decorated in a restrained and tasteful style. Nothing too bright or harsh on the eye. I get to work.

Chapter Nineteen

The gardens are a scene of great revelry. Apart from the music, dancing, costumes and fine provisions on offer, there are spectacular lighting effects and frequent appearances of otherworldly creatures. The genteel crowds, thinking these to be part of Lisutaris's sorcerous entertainment, are enchanted.

It seems that only Makri and I realise the danger. Makri tries to prevent the creatures from doing too much damage, which leads to the odd sight of a woman in Orcish armour walking round the gardens being followed by a long line of centaurs and unicorns. Centaurs, lascivious creatures at the best of times, can't help being attracted to Makri—I saw it happen in the fairy glade—and while Makri does her best to shoo them away, they continue to follow her until the magic which has produced them becomes unstable and they fade into space. As for the unicorns, I don't know why they should take to her. It's not like she's pure of heart.

"I've never seen anything like it," says a wealthy-looking pirate to his companion as a rather harassed Makri jogs past with a long line of mythical beasts in close pursuit. "Lisutaris has really laid on the entertainment."

A bolt of blue lightning cracks the sky overhead.

"She's the best Sorcerer in the city!" enthuses the pirate.

Meanwhile I'm looking for pendants. This is not so easy because Lisutaris's bracelet keeps lighting up any time a naiad or mermaid appears. With so many false alarms it's difficult to concentrate. When I notice two Makris at opposite ends of the gardens, one with unicorns and one without, I sprint towards the lone figure. I have a feeling that Makri's imitator has something to do with all this. Seeing my approach, the figure flees into the bushes and I follow. Immediately I step into the undergrowth my bracelet lights up. There's a man in a bishop's costume bending down in the shadows to pick something up. I leap for him and wrestle the object out of his hands.

"That's mine!" says the bishop.

I shove the pendant into my bag. He lets go with some language very unsuitable for a man of the cloth.

"You'll thank me later," I say, and hurry on. Some success at least. I find another pendant in a fountain full of mermaids and another in the hands of a Palace official who, while talking wildly about the coup he is planning to stage, is at least not yet dead. I retrieve the pendant and leave him to sleep off his dreams of power. I now have three pendants, but from the way a comet is currently hovering over the gardens, I'd say there were still more to be collected.

"Why did they all end up here?" I say out loud, angry and puzzled.

"I'm partly responsible," says an elegant voice at my shoulder. It's Horm the Dead, dressed as a mythical King of the Depths, complete with trident.

"I figured you would be."

"It wasn't my original plan," confesses Horm. "When I finally got my hands on the pendant I intended to leave the city. Unfortunately I then located a second pendant and realised that someone had been duplicating them. In the past day I've come across rather a lot of them."

"So you sent them all to Lisutaris's ball?"

"It seemed like the helpful thing to do."

Horm laughs.

"I have always wished to see what would happen when so many unsuitable sorcerous elements were brought together. With luck we may all disappear in an explosion which will flatten the entire city. Look above. The stars are multiplying in the sky."

They do seem to be. A million extra points of light. The points grow larger, resolving into a vast shower of comets heading our way. They start raining down on the garden, each one tiny and brightly coloured. The guests applaud wildly.

"This is splendid," enthuses Horm. "Everyone is about to die and they are all applauding. And you have the task of gathering pendants in a bag! Really, I've never seen anything so funny."

There's a movement in the bushes and Makri appears. Or rather, a woman in Orcish armour. I can tell immediately it's not Makri. My senses go into overdrive as the woman pulls a pendant from her pocket and holds it towards me.

"Not so fast, Sarin!" I cry, and strike her so she falls heavily to the ground. I grab the pendant from her hands and thrust it in my bag.

"You think you can just wave a pendant in my face, do you?"

I rip off her mask and stick my face close to hers. Unfortunately it is not Sarin. It's Princess Du-Akai, the highest-ranking woman in all of Turai, third in line to the throne.

"Excuse me, Princess Du-Akai. There has been a misunderstanding."

There's no way I'm talking my way out of this one. You can't strike a royal princess and get away with it. I'm heading for a prison galley.

"I was swimming with the dolphins," mumbles the Princess, and looks confused.

Of course. She's been looking at the pendant. She doesn't realise what's happening. Thank God for that. Unless she dies. That won't be so good. I put her down gently. Horm the Dead is laughing so much he can hardly catch his breath. Not wishing to leave the Princess close to the malevolent Sorcerer, I cram her helmet back on her head, hoist her over my shoulder and march towards the house.

"Look after this woman," I instruct a group of household servants. "She's been drinking too much and needs to sleep it off."

I am now completely fed up with everything. There seems to be no end in sight to this madness. There might be forty of these pendants scattered around here for all I know. I notice that some of the guests are now looking nervous as a new flock of centaurs stampede through a marquee and show less willingness to dematerialise, even when Makri threatens them with her swords. Lisutaris appears to quickly banish them by sorcery but it's clear things are getting out of hand.

"It bit me!" complains a woman loudly to Lisutaris.

I need to know how many pendants there are. It's time to threaten someone. I look around for the most senior household servant I can find.

"I have to find Lisutaris's secretary right now. What costume is she wearing?"

"That would be a breach of etiquette, I'm afraid—"

I offer him a bribe. He looks uninterested. I take him by the neck and push him against the wall, ignoring the consternation this causes among his fellow servants.

"Spill it."

"She's wearing a wood nymph's costume with yellow flowers!"

Now I've assaulted a princess and threatened Lisutaris's staff. Not forgetting the spell I worked on Captain Rallee. The courts may have to invent some new sort of punishment to deal with my vast catalogue of crime.

I start hunting the gardens for a wood nymph with yellow flowers. Makri spots me and hurries to my side.

"Have you got all the jewels yet? No? You'd better hurry, things are getting out of hand. There are centaurs everywhere and they keep trying to chew my clothes off."

"Centaurs are like that. Any deaths?"

"Maybe one or two. You want me to keep count for our bet?"

"No, I was just wondering how things were going. But now you mention it, keep a count anyway. I'm looking for Avenaris. I figure she can tell me how many jewels there are."

"Lisutaris will be down on you like a bad spell if you bother her secretary."

"I already searched her rooms."

"You did?"

"I did. And found various Barius-related items. She's been snuggling up with Professor Toarius's son. And no doubt funding his dwa habit after his father cut him off."

I tell Makri about Princess Du-Akai. Makri is annoyed to hear that a royal princess has been masquerading as an Orcish gladiator.

"I'm insulted."

"That's not the point. The point is I hit the Princess. If she remembers I'll be executed."

"We could fight our way out."

"We might have to. Now help me look for Avenaris."

By now the masked ball has become a fantastic affair of flashing illuminations and rampaging sorcerous beasts. It's fabulous entertainment. I'd stop to enjoy it if I didn't know the city was going to explode any minute. It's difficult working our way through the crowds. Even among the garishly dressed revellers Makri's unusual costume draws attention. My funny Cicerius mask gets a few smiles too, though not from Cicerius himself when I bump into him outside the green marquee. He stares balefully at me and I can see him trying to work out where he's seen this large figure before.

"Wood nymph with yellow flowers over there," yells Makri, and we set off in pursuit.

We catch up with Avenaris near the orchard.

"Don't be too harsh with her," suggests Makri.

A great blast overhead signals the arrival of another shower of small meteors, which thud into the ground around us.

"No time to be nice," I grunt. I grab Avenaris, shove her into the darkness beneath the trees and rip my mask off.

"I need some answers and I need them right now."

Avenaris shrinks back.

"Go away," she pleads.

I point to the lights in the sky.

"You see all this? It's getting out of control and it's going to end in disaster unless I recover every duplicate pendant. So tell me how many there are."

The secretary starts crying. Tears pour from under her mask. I take out my sword.

"There are dead people here already. Tell me what I want to know or I'll kill you right now."

"Help me!" wails Avenaris to Makri.

Makri draws her black Orcish sword.

"Sorry," she says. "It's time to talk."

Avenaris slides down the trunk of a tree till she's sitting with her back to it, looking like a child. She sniffs, and takes off her mask.

"I didn't know all this was going to happen. I gave Barius the jewel. He needed money."

"I know. For dwa. Bad choice for a boyfriend."

"He said he would give it back. He was going to copy it and sell the copy. I didn't know he would make so many."

"How did he make the copies?"

"I stole a spell," sniffs Avenaris. "From Lisutaris's private library. Barius took it to a Sorcerer's apprentice he knows."

"You realise the danger you've put everyone in?"

Avenaris looks miserable, but whether it's due to the trouble she's caused I'm not sure. She might just be sad about her boyfriend's problems.

"It was very disloyal to Lisutaris," says Makri, disapprovingly.

Avenaris raises her head. A strange expression flickers across her face. I can't read it exactly, but for a moment she looks almost defiant.

"I should have been the rich one," she says. "My father was head of the family."

She lowers her head and looks pathetic again.

"How many pendants did he make?"

"Fifteen. Then the spell wouldn't work any more."

"I have nine pendants in my bag. Lisutaris has three. That's twelve. Four more to collect."

"Three more," says Makri, and takes one from her purse.

"You found one? And didn't stare into it?"

"I have will power."

We hurry off, leaving Avenaris crying under the trees. Three pendants to find, which quickly becomes two as we stumble across the body of a young man who's still clutching one between his fingers. I scoop it into my bag. I hope that the red Elvish cloth will contain them as effectively as Lisutaris claims.

"Will the city really be flattened?" asks Makri.

"It's possible."

"But I've got an examination tomorrow. And I really studied hard for it."

A unicorn trots out from the trees. They're pleasant animals. I never thought I'd get so sick of seeing them. It approaches Makri and starts nuzzling her face.

"I just don't see why these unicorns like you so much. It's not like you're a virgin."

"Is that an insult?" says Makri, suspiciously.

"No, just a statement of fact."

"I'm sure that virginity has nothing to do with it anyway," says Makri, patting the unicorn. "It's my sunny personality. Or maybe it's the Elvish blood. Is this actually a real unicorn?"

"I don't know. It doesn't show any sign of disappearing. Neither does that mermaid who's hypnotising the man in a sailor's costume. Come on, we have two pendants to find."

My bracelet starts glowing. I climb into the fountain, bat the mermaid out of the way and scoop up another pendant. Only one more to go.

Lisutaris, in her splendid angel costume, arrives in the company of someone who might be Prince Frisen Akan. His costume is rich enough for a prince, and he's drunk, so it could be. On seeing us Lisutaris sends him gently on his way and asks about our progress.

"One more to go."

"Are you sure only one is missing?"

"Yes."

"Then we are finished," proclaims the Sorcerer. "I have it. I found it with two Senators who'd taken it off a unicorn. They were about to fight. Fortunately I interrupted them before their venal dreams could drive them mad or kill them."

Lisutaris breathes a great sigh of relief.

"I'm glad that's all over. Thing were becoming hectic. I had to banish a troop of mountain trolls who were eating all the food, and the Consul got tangled up with an angry dryad. Unless that was just an angry citizen, it's been hard to tell."

We withdraw under the privacy of a clump of trees. It's a hot night and sweat is running down my face beneath my mask. Makri removes her helmet to wipe her brow. Lisutaris takes the bag of pendants, adds the jewels to the contents she already has, then rummages around inside. After a few moments she draws out a jewel.

"This is the real one."

"How can you tell?"

"I'm head of the Sorcerers Guild."

"You were fooled by an imitation before."

"I didn't have the rest to compare then. Besides, I had to show the Consul something."

I take the pendant in my hand. It seems the same as all the others. But you have to trust Lisutaris on matters like this. She's number one chariot in all matters of sorcery. I hand it back.

"Congratulations," comes a familiar voice. It's Horm the Dead, still in costume.

Lisutaris greets him coldly.

"I do not believe I invited you."

"I did not wish to miss such a glittering occasion. Or the chance of meeting Makri again."

He bows to Makri, who looks uncomfortable, and may be blushing. In the shadow of the trees it's hard to tell. Horm looks at the pendant in Lisutaris's hand.

"You know, I went to some trouble to send these all to your ball. Some I retrieved by sorcery . . . Casax for instance seemed unwilling to hand his over to me—some I bought, which involved rather large payments to Sarin—some I acquired from people I . . . removed."

"Tough luck," I say. "Your plan failed."

"My plan?"

"To cause such sorcerous instability that a disaster happened."

"Yes," agrees Horm. "That would have been excellent. But that was not exactly my plan. Merely an entertaining lie. I still intend to take the pendant back to Prince Amrag. Till they were all gathered together, I could not be certain which was the original. And since you, Lisutaris, had already managed to retrieve one of the pendants, I felt that here would be as good a place as any to bring them all together. And now you have picked out the real one for me."

"Your power does not equal mine, Horm the Dead."

"You are mistaken. It does. But we do not have to battle each other now. You will simply hand over the original pendant to me and I will not drop this handful of powder on your bag."

"What?"

"My own preparation. It will rot the red Elvish cloth in a matter of seconds. Unprotected by the magical barrier provided by the cloth, the fifteen pendants in close proximity to each other will, I believe, cause a sorcerous event of such magnitude that few of your guests will survive."

Horm turns his head towards me.

"Please do not try any sudden movement. I am quite prepared for it, and you will die. Lisutaris, the pendant."

We seem to be stuck. It's the sort of moment a man needs to think of a quick plan. I don't come up with anything. Horm lets a little dust trickle from his fingers. The Elvish cloth starts to decay before our eyes.

"You will still have a fake jewel for fooling the Consul," says Horm, and holds out his hand. Lisutaris has no choice. Everyone here will die. She hands over the original. Horm tucks the pendant into the folds of his costume and then, unexpectedly, he removes his mask. He moves a step closer to Makri and leans towards her, quite slowly. He kisses her lightly on her lips. Makri doesn't move at all. Horm steps back.

"You will one day visit my Kingdom," he says, before turning on his heel and hurrying off, leaving Makri looking embarrassed.

Horm doesn't get far. A masked figure steps swiftly out from behind a tree with a short club in his hand and slugs Horm on the back of the head. Horm crumples to the ground. It's nice work. Moving swiftly, the figure reaches down to wrench the pendant from Horm's grasp.

"Good work, Demanius," I say.

The masked figure looks over in surprise.

"I recognised the clubbing action. Now give the pendant to Lisutaris and we'll get rid of Horm."

The Investigator draws his mask up, revealing his features.

"Can't do that, Thraxas. I'm working for Rittius at the Palace. The pendant goes to him."

"That's ridiculous."

"I'm not paid to argue."

It's intolerable. We go through all this and the pendant still isn't coming home. I'm still trying to work through the ramifications of Demanius returning the pendant to Rittius at Palace Security when the Investigator makes to leave.

"Stop him," cries Lisutaris.

Demanius, almost at the edge of the trees, jerks backwards. For a moment I think that Lisutaris has halted him with a spell. Then, as his body spins and falls, I notice a crossbow bolt sticking from his chest. Another masked figure, tall and slender, darts from behind the tree. She grabs the pendant and leaps into the crowd, disappearing immediately among the throng. Sarin the Merciless. I wondered where she'd got to.

Chapter Twenty

"You didn't find her?"

Makri arrives in Lisutaris's private chambers some time after the death of Demanius. She shakes her head.

"She's a slippery woman, Sarin. Probably climbed the outside wall while you were still searching the marquees."

"I didn't see you rushing to help," complains Makri, and sits down heavily on a gilded couch.

"I've done enough rushing around."

Lisutaris herself is sitting dejectedly on another couch.

"You still have a lot of fakes," says Makri.

"They'll spot it at the Palace. I can't believe we lost the pendant after we went to so much trouble."

I'm sorry about Demanius. He was a good man. His body

has been removed discreetly by Lisutaris's staff and now lies in a cellar, along with another two unfortunate souls who met their end as a result of the pendants. Two dead guests. Not as bad as it could have been. Lisutaris can probably explain it away as natural causes. The way some of these elderly Senators have been drinking and dancing, you'd expect a few fatalities.

I take a bottle of wine from under my toga.

"Help yourself to my supplies," says Lisutaris.

"I figure I earned it."

I'm tempted to demand an explanation for my not being invited to the ball. It still rankles. I swallow it back. No need to hear Lisutaris explain in detail that I'm just not the right class of person.

"You know that this whole thing was started off by your secretary?"

"So you say."

"I don't just say. I know. I searched her rooms. You'd be surprised what I found there. Letters to Barius. A diary full of some interesting observations about you. And a few items she's probably stolen from you over the years. Didn't you suspect her at all?"

"I told you to leave her out of this."

"You know she resents you for inheriting the family fortune? It wouldn't surprise me if she blames you for her father's death."

Lisutaris glares at me.

"Thraxas. Do you think that this is unknown to me? Do you seriously believe it has never crossed my mind that my brother's daughter may be jealous of my position? That she may have acted unwisely out of resentment at me inheriting the bulk of the family's wealth?"

"Well shouldn't you be doing something—"

The Sorceress raises her hand.

"I am doing something. I'm protecting her. I have a duty to my family. You will not mention her part in this to anyone and you will not raise the subject with me again. Count yourself fortunate that I do not punish you for searching her room."

I shrug. If Lisutaris wants to wake up one day with a knife in her ribs, courtesy of her disgruntled niece, that's her problem.

"You hired me to get the pendant. So I did what I had to do. It's my job."

"You failed."

Poor Lisutaris. Downstairs her ball is a raging success and here she is, slumped on a couch smoking thazis and looking as miserable as a Niojan whore. It's a tough life as head of the Sorcerers Guild.

"Failed? Me? Failure is an alien concept to Thraxas the Investigator."

I take the real pendant out of my bag.

"Number one chariot at investigating, as is commonly said."

Lisutaris leaps off the couch to grab the pendant.

"How did you get this?"

"I palmed it, of course, when you were showing it off. I made a switch right under your nose. It's the sort of thing I do well."

"But why?"

"Why? You think I was going to let you keep the pendant when the gardens were full of people like Horm and Sarin? It was asking for trouble."

"Couldn't you have told me that before I went chasing after Sarin?" says Makri.

"You ran off too quickly. You're impetuous, Makri, I've mentioned it before. Anyway, you wanted to kill her and I wasn't going to stand in your way. Don't worry, you'll get another chance."

Lisutaris, no longer as miserable as a Niojan whore, congratulates me.

"I have the pendant. I have all the fakes. The one Sarin took will destabilise and disappear soon. I'm in the clear!"

"You are indeed. Unfortunately, I'm not. I'm in trouble for not answering a summons from Palace Security."

"I can have that rescinded," says Lisutaris.

"I put a Guards captain to sleep with a spell."

"I can probably smooth that over," says Lisutaris.

"I hit Princess Du-Akai."

"You're in big trouble," says Lisutaris. "I could act as character witness."

The sorcerer offers me some thazis and I accept it gratefully. As I inhale the pungent smoke I can feel my body relaxing.

"And what," asks Lisutaris, turning to Makri, "is the idea of kissing Horm the Dead?"

"I didn't kiss him. He kissed me."

"I didn't see you putting up much of a struggle."

Makri looks embarrassed again.

"He took me by surprise."

Lisutaris fails to look convinced.

"I was expecting you to punch him."

"I tried that already," says Makri. "It didn't seem to put him off."

Lisutaris frowns.

"I can see he's quite good looking in a pale, high cheekboned sort of way, Makri, but really you ought to be careful. You don't want to go around getting involved with someone like Horm. You know it's rumoured he's already been dead?"

"Thraxas mentioned it," mutters Makri, and starts inhaling

deeply from the water pipe, not wishing to discuss it any further.

"Well, he's gone now," continues Lisutaris. "I scanned the gardens. If he comes back I recommend staying well clear of him."

"He offered Makri a position as captain of his armies," I tell her.

"Really?"

"Could we just stop talking about this now?" says Makri crossly.

We let the matter drop. I suppose if some insane sorcerer takes a shine to Makri it's not really her fault, though it might not happen if she could learn to dress properly. A man like Horm, living out in the wastelands, he's bound to be affected when he hits the city and the first thing he runs into is Makri in her chainmail bikini.

I leave Makri and Lisutaris fuelling up with thazis before they go off to enjoy the rest of the ball. ·I've had enough excitement and decide to head home. In the hallway of the house I run into Deputy Consul Cicerius.

"You are Thraxas, I believe," he says acidly.

"I am. But about the mask, it was the only one I could find in a hurry—"

"I am not concerned with your grotesque likeness of me. I am concerned with your treatment of Princess Du-Akai."

Here it comes. Thraxas heads for prison ship.

"She tells me that she was assailed in the gardens by a unicorn and you rescued her. Is this true?"

The Princess is suffering from some very garbled memories.

"Yes, it's true. But I don't want to make too much of it. It was very dangerous but anyone would have done the same."

"Nonetheless, it was a spirited action. Some of Lisutaris's

entertainments have been far too adventurous. I am furious that our royal princess was endangered."

The Deputy Consul is one of the city's strongest supporters of the royal family. He's really grateful to me.

"Do you think I could have my Investigator's licence back?" I ask.

"Yes," says Cicerius. "I will arrange it."

"Can you have the charge of throwing away my shield dropped?"

"Unfortunately not. That must go through its due process. You were mistaken about Praetor Capatius. It was not he who initiated the charge. It was Professor Toarius. He was endeavouring to prevent you from investigating his son."

"That figures. You know his son's a dwa addict who's heading for trouble?"

Cicerius declines to comment. As I leave him he's looking on with distaste at some dancing girls who are probably Senator's daughters, but aren't behaving appropriately. Or maybe they are behaving appropriately. Senators' daughters are notoriously corrupt.

Next afternoon I'm sitting downstairs in the Avenging Axe. Gurd is beside me at the table, laboriously writing a letter to Tanrose. He's finding it difficult.

"I've never written a letter before."

"It'll be fine. Put in more compliments. Tell her that Thraxas is getting thin."

"She won't believe that."

I encourage Gurd to get on with repairing his relationship with the cook. Neither of us can carry on without her.

I'm fairly satisfied with events. Most things worked out well enough. I did good service, for which Lisutaris is grateful, and the Deputy Consul is back on my side. The only bad thing is that I'm still faced with a charge of cowardice dating back seventeen years. I wonder if Professor Toarius will pursue it, now his son has been exposed. He wanted to prevent me from investigating, but now that the truth has come out about his son's behaviour anyway, perhaps he'll drop it. I sigh. Dwa addicts. They lose all responsibility. Prepared to steal five gurans from a locker or one of the most valuable items in the city. It makes no difference to them.

I'm keeping an eye on the next table, where young Moxalan, surrounded by onlookers, is working things out on sheets of paper. Calculating how many deaths actually occurred as a result of the case of the missing pendant is a tricky business. There were fatalities all over the city, many of which could be ascribed, directly or indirectly, to the pendants.

The front door flies open and Makri strides dramatically into the room. She flings her bag on the floor, drags her tunic over her head and throws it at the wall, then starts parading round in her chainmail bikini, arms aloft, a look of triumph on her face. I've never seen her behave quite like this. It must be something she learned to do in the gladiator pits after slaughtering her enemies.

Makri marches round the room, arms still in the air, grinning arrogantly, so that people start applauding even though they don't know what for.

"Makri!" she says eventually. "Number one chariot at examinations!"

"You passed?"

"Passed? 'Passed' doesn't do my performance justice. I set new standards. Never has a class been declaimed to in such an authoritative manner. The students were awestruck. When I finished my speech they stood up and cheered."

Gurd grins. Dandelion, still in residence, brings Makri a beer to celebrate. I congratulate her warmly.

"Well done. I knew you'd pass."

"It was a triumph," she enthuses. "Not even Professor Toarius could say a word against it. I tell you, I was great. And all this on no sleep. You know I spent the whole night dancing at the ball? It was the social event of the season. Lisutaris has been widely complimented. I walked from her house to college this morning and did my examination. I'm now sailing into my final year as top student. Incidentally, word got round about Barius. No one now thinks I'm a thief."

A good day all round. And it might get better. Moxalan is ready to make his announcement.

"With the help of my fellow adjudicators," he announces, "I proclaim that the final death total in the case of Thraxas and the missing pendant is sixty-three."

There are groans from all round the room. No one seems to have picked this total. Moxalan's eye glints greedily.

"No winners at sixty-three? Then we move on to the reduced-odds winner for closest bet. Anyone with sixty-two? No? Sixty-one? Sixty?"

"Me!" yells Makri, leaping to her feet once more. "I have sixty." She retrieves her bag from the floor and hunts for her ticket.

"I'm not happy at this," complains Parax the shoemaker. "She had inside information."

Many suspicious eyes are turned on me. I splutter in protest.

"Makri had no inside information from me. I have remained aloof from the entire contest, thinking it to be in the poorest of taste. I am disgusted with all of you and will now retire upstairs to forget I ever met any of you."

I leave with dignity, and beer.

A while later Makri appears upstairs, still on a high after her examination triumph. She starts counting out her bag of money, splitting it three ways for herself, Lisutaris and me.

"Twenty to one, not bad. We lost a lot of stake money on our first bets but we've still got a good profit. This will get me started at college next year. That was a good wager, Thraxas. You picked sixty, it was well worked out."

"I'm sharp as an Elf's ear. Incidentally, did you tell Lisutaris last week that she shouldn't invite me to her ball because I really didn't like that sort of thing?"

"No," says Makri, sharply. "Why would you think that?"

"Investigator's intuition."

"Well your intuition is quite mistaken. It's not all you make it out to be, you know. Here, take this pile of money. It'll make you feel better."